The Ragged Edges

1930

Ladies of Bottlebrush Grove Series

Olwyn Harris

Peace I leave with you,
My peace I give unto you:
Not as the world giveth,
Give I unto you.
Let not your heart be troubled,
Neither let it be afraid.

(John 14: 27)

Published by: Reading Stones Publishing
Helen Brown & Wendy Wood
Woodwendy1982.wixsite.com/readingstones
Cover Design: Olwyn Harris - Some of the cover elements were created using AI technology.

For more copies contact the publisher at:
Glenburnie
212 Glenburnie Road
ROB ROY NSW 2360
Mobile: 0422 577 663
Email: Readingstonespublishing@gmail.com

I.

"Nurse!" The doctor swore as he saw the life pass out of his patient's eyes. "I am going to have to take the baby. Or we will lose him too. Now! Pass me the scalpel." He deftly made the cut. The doctor plunged his arm into her womb and extracted the baby. He pulled out a slippery mite. A girl. Blue. No breath. He quickly tied the cord and snipped her free. It was hardly necessary in the warmth of the November evening, but he took her over to the stove where it radiated stifling and hot. He grabbed a chair and placed her on his knee face down. "Come on little one," he coaxed, vigorously massaging her back, draining the fluids from her lungs. "Come on! God in Heaven, not the child too. Damn it! Breathe!" He flipped her over and gently puffed his breath into her mouth. Again. Again. And then, as if there was a command from the Heaven he petitioned, she opened her eyes and bellowed.

Sister Blaine came and took the baby from his arms, swaddling her firmly in a clean wrap as the doctor sat hard against the stiff hardback kitchen chair. He closed his eyes, loosened his collar in the heat, removed his kerchief from his pocket, and took off his spectacles to clean them. Then he wiped his mouth, sticky from the baby, looked at his kerchief and put it back in his jacket as he surveyed the room. It had the look of a massacre, not the work of a healer. He went over and gently covered the mother's body in a sheet. Then he sighed and took a deep breath as he pulled it back and stitched up the incision. Suddenly fatigue reached in a squeezed his heart, and he felt his chest tighten as sweat beaded on his brow. "Getting too old for this," he murmured, and started to stack his things in a basin on the bench. "Nurse, I'll take the baby. See if you can clean her up. I don't want her husband coming in and seeing this."

Sister Blaine nodded and indicated the crib that had been set up in the corner of kitchen near the stove. Doctor Mortimer looked at it but sat on the chair, holding her gently. The miracle of life and the tragedy of death were two extremes he never got used to. It was always more confronting when they happened simultaneously. He studied her little face, crinkled and caked with blood and whispered a prayer. "God in Heaven, protect this little one... give her peace... because her start in this life has been anything but."

The nurse worked quickly, washing her body, changing her nightgown. The soiled linens piled up. She was mopping the floor when they heard steps on the verandah. Sister Blaine glanced at the doctor, and he nodded as he stood up. The door opened, and he stood there. Everything slowed to a series of snapped black and white photographs. The man in the doorway took in the covered sheet on the table in the middle of the room. He stared at the doctor standing by the stove, rocking a bundle of wraps, with a penetrating look of sympathy. He glanced past the nurse, who stood holding a mop, to a bundle of linens, an inkblot of blood seeping through. He said nothing but turned around and left. Then they heard a blood curdling guttural bellow from the blanket of darkness outside. It went on and on.

* * *

2.

The nurse finished mopping the floor and then tipped the bucket of water out by the fence. She looked into the shadows and saw Mr Galloway sitting on a stump by his shed. She put down the bucket and went over to him. In the pale moonlight of night, he sat still like stone. "Mr Galloway, I am sorry for your loss."

He said nothing.

"Dr Mortimer did everything he could. He saved your daughter's life."

He grunted. Growled.

"I know this is hard, but you have to consider your baby. I know a lady who has been nursing a baby while his mother has been sick. The mother is sufficiently recovered for the child to go back home. I could ask if she would take care of your daughter." Silence. She took a breath and plunged ahead. "This has to be sorted tonight, Mr Galloway. It can't be put off."

"Do whatever you think is best."

"Mr Galloway... this is your daughter. She is completely dependent on you. You must decide what is best."

He stood up and turned away. "Get the wet-nurse," he said curtly, and he walked away into the dark.

The midwife returned to the house. The doctor still held the baby, murmuring as he rocked her by the stove. "Doctor, are you starting to dote as you near your retirement? What ever happened to your stern reputation?"

"It's two o'clock in the morning; I just watched her mother die, and this little mite put up the fight of her life. I've listened to her father howl like a crazed dog at the moon. My heart is not made of stone."

She nodded. "I've known the secret of your kind heart for a long time. I am taking her over to Sal Frazer's. Mrs Martin doesn't need her services any further."

"Well, let's to it then. This night is done for anyway. No point disturbing Holmes or Reverend Mason until after we drop the baby off. And what about Flynn?"

"I spoke to him about Mrs Frazer. But other than that... he is in shock."

The small Galloway farm was on the edge of Lenwick township, but its long driveway gave the impression it was in the middle of nowhere. From there, it wasn't far to Sal's place, a rundown little cottage that creaked in the dark as if it had a life of its own. They knocked at the door. Three times.

"Who is it?" came the call from inside.

"It's Doc Mortimer. We have the Galloway baby."

She quickly opened the door and let them in. "Mrs Galloway?"

The nurse shook her head. "No. She didn't make it."

She gasped. "Oh. I am so sorry. And Mr Galloway... how is he?"

The nurse shook her head again. "Not great. As you would expect. But he was willing for you to care for the girl. She's about three weeks early. It is going to be touch and go." She handed the baby over to her.

Doc Mortimer shifted his weight. "I'll cover the costs... at least until after the funeral. That will give Mr Galloway some time to work out which way is up."

"Thank you, Doctor. That is generous."

“Hmm. Necessary, I think.”

“Well sure... okay.” She pushed aside the wraps and studied the little face of her charge. “Oh! What a little daisy! Pretty as a picture. I’ll take her, of course.”

* * *

3.

The parishioners filed out of the small country weatherboard church. Salome shook Reverend Mason's hand and stepped off the gravel path with the perambulator and pulled her two children, a girl and a boy, in beside her. They waited for the baby's father to emerge. "Mr Galloway? Mr Galloway, I was wondering..."

"Huh?" He looked confused but then registered the connection when the baby started fussing. "Oh. Right. You're the wet-nurse," he said with a curl to his lip.

Sal cringed at his tone, and picked the baby up, rocking her gently. "I truly am sorry for your loss Mr Galloway..." This was the first time he had actually paused long enough for her to offer her sympathies. Since the funeral, their brief contact had been like the westerly winds: hot, blustery and uncomfortable.

"Suppose you can call me Flynn... since you are nursing the baby."

"Yes, I am, Mr Galloway. Nursing your baby. Yours."

He looked impatient. "What is it that you want?"

"Um... We agreed we would meet so you could have some time with her. Remember? You haven't held her at all since she was born." She reached out to pass her over, but he stepped back.

"I told you I have to go back to work. I have work... which is more than most around here. I will be home on the fortnight... maybe three weeks. We can talk then." She had not moved. "What else is there?" he said abruptly.

"You are not going to see her for Christmas?"

"She will not know whether I am there or not. I have to be at work, so others can..." His voice cracked, and he swallowed.

"Oh. Well... as long as I know. I just needed to check everything was to your satisfaction."

He stared at her and grunted. Could she really think anything at all was satisfactory? He turned to go.

"Mr Galloway, one other thing. What is her name? I don't remember you telling me what you have named her."

"Huh. Don't know."

"You must know what you want to call her. What about her mother's name?"

"Joy? I ain't calling her that. It would be a lie."

"That is your prerogative Mr Galloway. Please think on it and let me know what you choose."

"Like I said, I'm going back to camp tomorrow. Just keep her with you."

"Don't you want to spend the afternoon with her? She must get to know her father."

He grunted. "Like I said, she won't know any difference. She'll get to know me soon enough, no doubt. I don't have time this afternoon. I have to get ready to leave." He turned to go and then stopped. "Oh Nurse..."

"My name is Salome. Silent 'e'. Or you can call me Sal."

"That's... unusual."

"It means Peace."

"Humph. Still odd. Just so you know, since I'm back at work, you will get your fee... I know the Doctor has been... well, you know... supplementing..."

She looked at his retreating back with a frown on her brow. It was a most unsatisfactory interview to have with a parent. But she often dealt with difficult situations. She shook her head bewildered and turned to the tiny narrow face in her arms encircled in a tiny white bonnet. "You are a sweet one, my bright little daisy. And Daisy... I disagree... I think you are a joy. I have grand hopes for you, Little One. Grand hopes," she whispered. "Little Daisy Hope."

* * *

Salome pushed open the door and maneuvered the wicker pram inside. Faith and Philip had already disappeared into a game, squabbling over who was going to take the lead on their next adventure which included climbing the tree in the back yard. They had salvaged some fence palings and built a platform to create a tree house. The bread dough had risen while they were gone, and Sal stoked the fire and slid the loaf tin into the oven. The baby was fussing, and she settled in a chair to feed her. This was her quiet place... a centre-point that offered Sal harmony, and calm, and nurture... even when those she nursed fretted and fussed. There was something about feeding a baby that was a precious moment to hold onto, in a world that was generally too busy, discordant and sparce. Philip ran in and dumped a bird's nest on the table. Little Philip didn't stop until he slept. "We found a sparrow's nest!" he announced as he disappeared out the front door without pausing. Salome shook her head with a smile as she looked at his line-up of dubious curiosities. His collectables were not clean, but they created stimulating conversation.

Just then Philip returned just as quickly, dumping an envelope beside her. "It was on the doorstep," he bellowed as he careered back through the house.

She considered it with raised brows. She didn't recognise the handwriting on the front, but it had an official look. When Dr Mortimer paid her, he did it in person, and he checked-over the little one at the same time. This envelope was not from him. She tore the seal on the paper. It was a short letter. She flicked open the folds with one hand and started to read as the baby continued to suckle.

She frowned. And then gasped. *Who delivers a letter like this on a Sunday? On her doorstep of all things! How dare they! Doesn't the Sabbath mean anything anymore? Could they not leave it until Monday morning and give it to her in person?*

It was a reminder of her failure to meet the payments agreed to when she signed the promissory note. The content of the letter seeped into her bones, and she felt her world sway and teeter dangerously. This house, and the land it was on... this was all she had. When Pedro died... after his sickness, this was what was left. Meagre. Inadequate. But hers none the less. She called out to the children. "Was there anything else with this on the porch? Or in the mailbox?"

Faith appeared with a frown and shook her head. "It was just there with a rock on it. Are you okay Ma'ma?"

"I am, my Sweet. As soon as I am finished feeding little Daisy, we will have lunch."

"Daisy? Is that her name now?"

"Well, she is a sweet little daisy... and I know her mother liked them, so I think for now that is what we will call her... until we get the official name."

"Huh. When I have a baby, I will name it straight up."

"Then you will make a wonderful mother. Were there eggs in the bird's nest you found?"

"I wanted to blow them, but Philip broke all three. He said it was by accident, but I reckon he didn't feel good about stealing their home while there were eggs in it."

"Hmm." It was a pity other people were not so conscience stricken. "Well... can you check the chooks and see if they have laid some eggs, and we will have them for dinner. Try not to break those."

There was an impatient knock at the door. She shook her head and unlatched the baby. Would they come now? Like vultures circling the weak. *"Oh God... don't let me sink! Pedro would say you helped his namesake, Peter walk through a storm on top of the water. And even when he was afraid and he started to sink, you fished him out."* That story had been like a badge of honour for Pedro. An excuse, maybe, to keep doing ridiculous and reckless things. But right now, she felt her wet feet and the storm waves crashing and the reality of it was drowning her. *"God, please keep the water firm, because this is swamping me."* She stood up and straightened her blouse. "Here Faith, hold the baby while I answer the door." Her daughter climbed into the worn armchair and held out her arms. There was another knock, pounding through her temples. "Coming!"

She opened the door and felt a moment of reprieve: it was not Mr Symanski, the Bank clerk, who stood there. But she was caught off guard. "Oh, it's you."

He grunted. "I think I need to apologise. I was short with you before."

"That is putting it politely Mr Galloway. You were very rude."

"My apologies. May I come in?"

Sal rolled her eyes, and stepped back, indicating for him to enter. He looked around. There was an unnatural slope in the middle of the floor where the floorboards sunk. The small room was not dirty, but the furniture was shabby and there was the clutter of baby things and children's toys, some of them broken. The basket of clean laundry on the kitchen table was waiting to be folded. He frowned at the collection of nature oddities lined up in a row on the table: the bird's nest, a cocoon, a dead rhinoceros beetle, a leaf skeleton and a piece of petrified wood.

She sighed and pursed her lips. "Why are you here? You were pretty clear that you would not see your baby until you return from the timber camp... *after* Christmas," she said pointedly.

"I... umm..." He cleared his throat. "I have animals. I need someone to look after them. I forgot that I... since..." He swallowed hard, and shook his head bewildered. "There used to be a neighbour who would check in on them, but they had to sell their place."

This was a common story, all over. People were going under. Sal was determined not to be one of them. She looked at him standing there, uncertain and uncomfortable, and felt disconnected and removed from his plight. She had her own matters crowding her mind just now. "And...?"

"And... I was wondering if you would do that. While I am gone. I will pay you extra."

"I can't be running out there twice a day to do your chores Mr Galloway. Not with a newborn baby, and two other children besides. And given I don't have either a horse and buggy, nor a motorcar to get there, I don't think that what you are asking is reasonable."

He frowned. "So, you can drive then?" That was unexpected.

"I do. But it is a moot point when I don't have a car." That was something else that had been sold.

He took a deep breath and ran his hand through his dark hair. "Oh. Yes. You are probably right. Sorry for bothering you." He turned to go.

Salome shook her head and relented. "Mr Galloway...? When I said I am sorry for your loss, I meant that sincerely. What if... maybe we could house-sit? That would solve the transport problem. Would that help? Just until you get back. I could ask Mrs Trimboli to look after my chickens."

He blinked in surprise. "You would do that? Stay out there?"

"Just this time, while you are away on your stint. That will, at least, give you an opportunity to find a more permanent solution."

"Oh. Well. Thank you."

"Well, you do live on a little farm... with animals. The kids will love it."

"Oh."

"It could be like a holiday for us. A Christmas holiday."

"Huh."

"And the extra money would be helpful, I don't deny it."

"Oh."

"Well. Okay then. You will have to tell me what is needed. We were just going to have lunch. Would you like to stay? You could hold your daughter while I get it ready." She didn't wait for him to answer but picked up the baby from Faith's arms. "Sit here..."

He didn't move, but continued to stand there awkwardly, frozen.

She paused, and then took the swaddled baby to him, and gently turning her little puckered face towards him. "Here little one... meet your Daddy..."

He swallowed hard and shook his head when she went to pass her over. "I... I can't."

"Well okay... I'll put her down. Perhaps you could rock the pram then."

He did not move.

"I have fresh bread, baked this morning. This is our Sunday treat. Do you like jam? We have some of Mrs Trimboli's apricot conserve. It is the best in Lenwick."

Flynn swallowed again and then nodded. Sal tucked the crocheted rug, that had been a gift from the minister's wife, around the baby. He looked cautiously into the pram as Salome gently snuggled her in there to sleep.

Philip was enlisted to remove his treasures, and he placed them carefully in a wooden box. "I'm sure he is going to be a naturalist, or a botanist, or an entomologist, or a geologist. Or a perhaps all of them. He has a curious little mind." Faith was given the task to set the table. "Faith has such a caring, nurturing little heart. It will not matter what work she does when she grows up, because she will bring care and compassion to whatever she chooses, and that will be so enriching. And since Faith is a peacemaker by nature, at the moment I am gunning for a role at the Prime Minister's office negotiating international armistices. Lord knows we need some competence on that scene. I wonder what breath-taking and remarkable things are in your little Daisy, that will come to light as she grows?"

Sal watched him closely in her peripheral vision as she set the sandwich fillings on the table, along with bread board. Flynn sat there stony and silent. He didn't register any objection to the use of Daisy as the baby's name. She gathered the children to sit, and they said grace. Then she guided Faith to cut her slice of warm oven bread, and then Philip was given the bread knife, his mother's hand on his... and he sawed his way through the loaf. "The bread tastes best straight from the oven, but it never cuts well when it is hot. So, if the choice is between precisely cut slices, stale from sitting around, or warm bread smelling wonderful but cut a little crooked, then Mr Galloway, my preference is for the ragged edges. I trust you will agree and forgive the lack of square crusts. We make our own sandwiches on Sunday." And they tucked in, demolishing the loaf of bread with gusto.

*　*　*

4.

Salome packed up some bags for the children and the baby, and threw them in the back of Flynn's cart, along with the pram. He had driven the horse and cart to her house that Sunday afternoon, leading his saddle horse tied to the tailgate. He had reverted to using his horses since he sold his truck. He even rode out to camp on horseback. The distracted frenzy of getting ready was a relief for Sal. Two or three weeks! Weeks away from the mess of home and the broken things that she never had the time or money to fix.

Salome had visited Flynn's wife, after they were newly married. Sal had admired her bashful wedding portrait; her first attempts at quilting which had looked near perfect; her vegetable garden fresh with seedlings, and her sparkling house that looked like it had stepped out of a catalogue. Sal's tour even included Joy's painting studio. It was a beautiful airy room surrounded with wide windows with an uninhibited view overlooking the paddocks towards the creek. Yes, her brand-new home was picture-perfect, but it was not child-friendly so she didn't come as often as she might have considered neighbourly.

Sal had gone away from that first visit more than a little jealous of Mrs Joy Galloway. Now... all she could think of was the stark tragedy of never nursing your own baby. Yes, Sal had lost her husband, but she still had the privilege of being a mother. That was something Joy Galloway would never know. Sal's little run-down cottage held something more precious than being a 'nice place'... it held memories of her children growing up.

When she told the children that their Christmas present this year was a holiday on a farm, Philip's eyes lit up like a lamp. "We will milk the cow... or the goat... and feed the pig; collect the eggs like we do at home. We can pick carrots from the garden, plant some flowers, pat the dog and maybe even ride the horse." It was an invitation to Heaven.

Early Monday morning they drove the cart out to the farm, past the sign, scripted in old-fashioned lettering, boarded with hand-painted bottlebrush flowers. The gate was surrounded with small sturdy bright red callistemon shrubs. It welcomed their arrival to "*Bottlebrush Grove*". They pulled up outside the house, hugged by a wide verandah all around. Sal paused before she opened the door. These walls had witnessed love in starting their life together, and then in such a short time, pain and loss at the other end. It felt wrong, in every way, invading another's home like this. These were indeed ragged edges.

It was the same with nursing other people's children. That was a ragged-edge type of thing as well. Having another woman wet-nurse your baby... that is something which is never meant to happen. But it is something that is needful when life takes a swing at you. Besides, you never know what you can do... until you have to do it. Never once did Salome think that this would be her calling: caring for another's baby while they sorted through what was going on in their life. There were the parents overwhelmed with sickness or had just checked-out... be it from pain, or the darkness of depression, or the storms of grief. Doc Mortimer brought her the first baby when Philip was still nursing, and she had more milk than five babies could drink. Since then, she had a steady stream of babies... and she protected her lactation like other people polished the tools of their trade. She was paid for the care, and the wet nursing was included. That was the unwritten arrangement, and the saving provision when Pedro died. She might be supporting other families by doing this… but it had supported her as well. There was something about having to nurture such a dependent life that forced her to put one foot in front of the other. This one thing had forced her to keep going.

Sal unloaded the cart, piled their bags and boxes on the verandah and lead the horse away to unhitch the cart. She had Faith rock the baby in the plain wicker pram, while she went out to survey the animals that were now in their charge. Philip helped her toss some hay into the horse yard, and then they had a quick look around. Bottlebrush Grove was indeed a wonderful place… even if it was just a small hobbyist affair. It wasn't what she considered to be a real farm.

The children were given instructions that when she clanged the cowbell, they were to come back in immediately. They ran outside squabbling about which fantastic thing they were going to explore first. Sal turned around slowly, taking in features of the house. The combustion stove was new, and the enamel on the firebox door was not stained with smoke. She admired the dining table, made from cedar wood, beautifully crafted, no scratches or marks. The living area was spacious, elegant, and tasteful. The mat even matched the cushions that were arranged on the lounge. Every wall had beautiful paintings, country scenes and flowers, all signed at the bottom, 'Joy'. One striking portrait was of an elderly gentleman with kind eyes. Sal smiled. She felt that man was inviting her to be his friend.

Sal stepped into the nursery. Mrs Galloway had attended to every detail; her baby's arrival prepared with anticipation. All around the cornice work there was a hand-painted frieze of a very sweet garland of daisies. It was barely started when she saw it last, but now it was finished. This had been part of the inspiration for Sal's intermediatory name for the baby. The linen on the shelves was white and yellow to match. The bassinet wicker was white, and the lemon wraps looked so cosy, delicate and refined. "Oh, little Daisy, your mother loved you well. It is very obvious that she did..."

She had a profound sense that Daisy was coming home. "Well, Little One," she said as she started unpacking the baby things from a box on the table, "We might be visiting, but you are home. And what a beautiful home you have little Daisy," she crooned, settling in for a feed in the soft lounge chair that had cushions that were not lumpy. "Don't worry Little One... he will come around. He is, after all, your Daddy."

Everywhere she looked, there were touches of Mrs Galloway. The embroidered doily on the sideboard. An unfinished matching fancywork project lay on the small occasional table near the lounge chair, that laid on top of a book that would never be finished. The arrangement of fine china in the hutch. The painting above the mantlepiece featured a large bowl of white chrysanthemums, also signed '*Joy*'. This had been a home, treasured and loved. But it had been left untouched like a shrine. It was very evident that the only places Mr Galloway had set his foot in his house, since that night Daisy had come to her care, had either been the kitchen or the bedroom. It didn't even look like he sat at the table. There were two rooms that didn't need little feet and fingers going through the things inside: the office and Mrs Galloway's painting studio. Joy went through the house with a box, filling it with nick-knacks, vases and ornaments that a couple of energetic children could carelessly knock, because they could not understand their value. She put that box in Joy's studio and declare it off limits.

The main bed was unmade, piled with shirts, trousers, a towel and other tossed items. Sal cleared them away, stripped the bed and made it up with fresh linen from the well-stocked linen press.

The day bustled into a scramble of finding things, and sorting things, and checking the list written down from Mr Galloway's instructions. They fed the pig, and the chickens, and the ducks, and the dog, and the dairy goat – which was obviously pregnant. Her stall had a sign with the name 'Spotty' decorated with a flattering goat-portrait. They checked the horse, and locked away the calf so they could milk the cow in the morning. She watered the vegetable garden and did some weeding. It took a while to settle, but they after a few days they had found a rhythm.

They went on an expedition, to chop down a small cypress pine and they stood it in the corner, propped in a bucket filled with gravel from the creek. They decorated their Christmas tree with all sorts of wonderful natural curiosities that they hung up with cotton. They found colourful Christmas beetles, their wings shimmering green in the sunlight, seedpods and feathers. They made little angels out of leaves, pods, paperbark, and twigs. The large star for the top of the tree was constructed from sticks and tied with more string. The weeks flew past in a swirl of horse rides, cow milking adventures and watching a clutch of eggs hatching baby chickens protected by a broody mother hen. Philip became devoted to Rusty, the dog, who did not go anywhere without him attached to his side.

They were sitting down for dinner, when the door opened, and Mr Galloway stood in the doorway. Their chatter froze in an awkward silence as he looked around his house, invaded by this messy, energetic family. He stared at the clumsy Christmas tree in the corner and the fine cypress pine needles that were dropping to the floor.

Sal stood to her feet. "Oh. Good evening, Mr Galloway. We didn't know exactly when you were coming back."

"Well, I'm here. Today. Evidently." He dumped his swag by the door and took off his hat and his boots.

"Yes. Evidently." She quickly cleared a spot. "Faith, please set Mr Galloway a place, and I will serve some dinner for him. How do you like your tea Mr Galloway?"

"Hot."

There was silence as Sal brought his plate to the table where he sat awkwardly, and then she paused, suspending the plate over his place, hovering like a dragonfly.

"What?" he said as he looked around the table. Both Faith and Philip stared at him in silent shock. "I live here... remember?"

Philip blurted out, "But you haven't washed up. Your hands are all dirty!"

He gaped at the boy in disbelief. "You have got to be kidding me."

"No," he said most seriously. "It is important to have clean hands and a kind heart... especially at dinner."

"Oh. Well. I will wash my hands. I guess."

Sal nodded and he took himself to the bedroom. He stood at the door looking at the tumble of sheets and blankets and the unpacked bags lined up along the wall in various states of disarray. This whole family had slept in his bed? He shook his head and took a breath. Okay. Washing up. He frowned at the array of soap and facewashes, toothbrushes and lotions on his washstand. He tipped out the used water and poured fresh water into the basin from the jug, gave himself a perfunctory glaze over with a washer, and scrubbed his hands. Then he maneuvered around the open suitcases on the floor by the wardrobe, pulled out a clean shirt and dragged it on quickly.

By the time he got back, his meal was set, the tea in his mug was hot. He sat down and looked at Philip and Faith. "Happy?" They nodded. "Okay. Anything else before I starve to death?"

"You have to say grace," said Faith seriously.

"Thank God for this food," he said looking directly at Faith without blinking. She was very dubious that such a statement could genuinely pass the grade. "Can I eat now?"

Faith shrugged and nodded.

Sal suppressed a smile. Daisy started stirring, so she directed the children to clear their plates and get ready for bed. She sat down with Daisy at the table and rocked her while she ate the last of her meal.

"Mr Galloway... this must be very difficult for you. Seeing other people in your house... especially at this time of year."

He didn't look at her but grunted. "The animals... did they survive?"

"They did. You have six newly hatched chickens. There were eight, but a hawk got a couple. We put them in the shed after that. I never actually thought about that being a problem. I think there is another hen going clucky now too. And the duck might be sitting too. The cow and goat are fine. The horse is exhausted from daily pony rides, and Rusty is becoming a devoted companion to Philip."

"It is probably best that he not to become too attached. What about the pig?"

"Pork Steaks?"

He choked on his food and put down his fork.

She gasped and reassured him quickly. "No... that is what we called it! The pig is fine. You didn't tell us her name. You don't seem to have a particular liking for names. We affectionately thought the name Pork Steaks would leave room for curing, if that is your plan."

"You call her Daisy," he said studying his carrots, as if the transition from naming the pig to naming his daughter was completely anticipated.

"I do. She has such a bright, fresh little face. What did your wife want to call her?"

He jolted. It took a while for him to answer. "She couldn't decide. She had a number of ideas. Daisy wasn't on her list."

"Oh...? Do you remember any of them?"

"Daphne was one name, I think. I like Daisy better."

Salome smiled and chuckled to the baby. "Did you hear that little Button? Daddy likes Daisy better than Daphne. This is progress. You will have a name very shortly, I am sure."

He shook his head. "It is also better than Button. Don't call her that."

Sal laughed. "Well good. I will continue to call her Daisy, until you give me the official word." She sobered then, and turned to him, as he drank his tea, unmoved. "Mr Galloway, I wondered if you had found a solution to your farm animal situation?"

"Haven't had time to think about it, much less sort it out. I have literally just ridden into town."

"I wanted to run an idea past you. You can let me know what you think before you need to go out to the camp again."

"Okay..."

"I would like you to help me save my family home."

"Your place?" he scoffed. His tone was disparaging.

"I know it has less street appeal than a rubbish tip, but that dump is mine. With their father gone, it is all that I have in this world to support my children. He wasn't a great husband as far as providers go, but I worked hard to have it free and clear. But when Pedro's health deteriorated so quickly and the doctors couldn't give us any answers, we had to mortgage it again to try the city doctors. I haven't been able to keep up the payments. They have given me two months to get it sorted. Realistically, they have been more than generous."

"Still don't see how I can help."

"I would like you to give me a loan... to satisfy the promissory note and the rates that are in arears, plus some labour-hire to fix the place up a bit. Then I'll be able to rent it. And I could stay here to look after your animals to pay your loan back. I know a family who will let it because they are after cheaper rent. With that money I will be able address the repayments. It would mean your daughter and your animals are looked after at no more cost than it is now."

"You want to move in here... while you rent out your place?" He looked around at the mess and thought it was a pretty poor reference.

"It means Daisy will have care, you will have a housekeeper, and someone to caretake your place while you are away... to look after your animals."

"You're not in the running you know."

"This plan will work. I absolutely need to save my family home. It makes no difference to me that it is less than dazzling. It is mine and that is important to me."

"I meant with me. You and me. That will never happen."

She blinked hard and flushed. "I wasn't asking to marry you! This is purely a way to keep my home. And let me assure you Mr Galloway, other 'benefits' are *not* included! My situation is like being measured up for a coffin while I am still breathing. People are losing their homes left, right and centre, and I don't want to be one of them. I need to be independent without bankers looking over my back fence."

He shook his head, unmoved. "I've got enough problems of my own, without bringing you into the picture. I'll find someone else to look after the animals."

"And what about your daughter? You need someone to look after her. We can help each other. I've thought this over long and hard, and nothing has come to mind except this plan."

"It is still a 'no'," he said unmoved. The idea of living with the chaos that these people brought with them wherever they went, was like a cat squalling outside his window at night. It put his teeth on edge. He didn't want to live with a perpetual toothache. He needed peace, and this was not it.

"Can you at least think about it? Daisy has been thriving in my care even though she was born early. Doc Mortimer is very pleased with her progress, and I have shown you I can look after your animals. This will save my family, and my home. But if it needs repeating, let me make myself perfectly clear: this plan does not include you in any way other than what I have stated. I've done the numbers. I only need the best part of a year. That is all I need to make it manageable again. By the time Daisy turns one and is ready to wean, I will leave regardless. I am not going to intrude on you courting someone else. Be assured, by the time your daughter is one year old, I will be gone, and you can happily get on with your life, with your new wife."

He stood up. Nothing about this situation was tempting. He had a cow, so he had milk. The baby would be fine. "I'll take the swag tonight since you have taken over my bedroom, and you leave in the morning."

"What are you saying? Does this mean you want me to leave Daisy here?" she asked bewildered. When he nodded, her eyes flew wide open. "Mr Galloway, you cannot intend to look after her yourself. You have not even held her!"

"I am her father. She is a Galloway. We will be fine."

"You might be fine, but she will absolutely not be okay. What will you do when you have to go back to camp? She is not livestock to be tossed a bale of hay. She is your baby daughter! That is a big difference. Please think about this sensibly Mr Galloway."

"You've made your point. But like you said, she is my daughter, and this is my decision. I will bring your payment into town tomorrow, as we agreed, and collect the cart." He stood up, and nodded, took the lamp down from the hook by the door and went outside to check his animals.

Sal watched him go with anger seething through her. How could someone, touched by such tragedy, be so hard? Joy had been such a blushing bride. But whatever Joy saw in him had died with her! Mr Galloway with his fine house, and his cutesy farm, was as much a pig as Pork Steaks!

* * *

5

Sal unpacked the suitcases and boxes and tidied her living room and did a load of washing. It didn't actually take long to create order without a baby to look after. It felt bare not having the baby in her arms. Philip and Faith had immediately checked their chooks and ran over to their neighbour to say hello. Now they were back climbing their tree and creating adventures in the back yard. Sal baked a batch of scones and took them outside in a basket that soon become part of their game. Faith threw her the end of a rope and Sal tied it around the basket handle so they could winch it up into their hideout. She went back inside, expressed her breast milk, and saved it in a boiled jar. She would take it over to Sister Blaine to distribute. She couldn't sell it of course, but sometimes a portion of sugar, or a little bit of flour, or a pumpkin would turn up on her step. It was also a way to let Sister Blaine know that she had a vacancy should another family need her services.

The wonderful three and a half weeks that had been their family farm holiday now seemed like an oasis in the barren reality of what was coming. Oh, how she resented the ragged edges just now. Sal sat down hard on the saggy lounge and shifted uncomfortably. She moved and extracted a hard kurrajong seed pod from where she was sitting. She put it to the side and held her head in her hands. "Oh God..." What a relief that she had read in her Bible that she didn't need words to pray; that the Holy Spirit was translating what was in her heart. If that was the case, the ache in her heart was one long prayer. As she pegged the clothes on the line, rinsed clean and tidily hung in a row, it reassured her that God could create order in her life again. What was dirty and crumpled would be made fresh and aligned and ordered. That offered her courage and confidence... even for Daisy Hope. She sincerely prayed peace over that family who had been ravaged by tragedy at its very inception.

But the afternoon came and went, and Mr Galloway had not appeared with her payment. As the next day progressed, she felt herself getting hotter and hotter. By that evening she was banging pots as she peeled and cut potatoes ready for dinner. The height of that man's arrogance! To think he figured she wanted to marry him! What a joke! The man was as dry as the dog bones that were scattered near Rusty's kennel. How long should she wait before she went back out there to demand payment on what she was owed? She settled the children at the table, and she spoke through gritted teeth to say grace. "Father God... we thank you for your provision." Amen to that. Provision. That was not just having sufficient potatoes for dinner. It was all the other stuff as well. Their house included.

There was an impatient knock at the door. "Who is it?"

"Flynn. Flynn Galloway."

She opened the door, less than impressed. "It is late. When you didn't turn up yesterday, I thought you had reneged on the payment you had agreed to. Then I expected you this morning. Your horse is around the back and I would appreciate..."

Mr Galloway stepped inside uninvited. He took off his hat. His face was ashen, and his forehead creased in a frown. He said nothing.

"Mr Galloway, is everything all right?"

"Ahh... no. Doc Mortimer asked me to come fetch you."

"Is it Daisy?"

He nodded.

"Oh." She grabbed her coat even as she was talking. "Kid's, I'm going over to the Doctors. Give Mr Galloway some potatoes. He looks like he hasn't eaten since yesterday. And a cup of tea... with sugar. Then come with him over to the infirmary. I will take your horse."

"I'm coming with you."

"Mr Galloway, I can't leave two small children here alone. That is what being a parent is. You have something to eat. And then bring them with you in the cart to Doctor Mortimer's. I will see you there." She left without pause.

He stared at the door as it closed firmly behind her. He turned around to see the large eyes of the children staring at him. "Humph. Guess we do what your mother said."

Philip led him to the table and pushed his mother's plate out of the way. Faith took a plate from the hutch and spooned a pile of mashed potato, that had the faint tinge of pumpkin through it, in the middle of the plate. She put it in front of him. She stared at him hard.

He obediently closed his eyes. "God. Thank..." What did he have to be thankful for? "Take care of Daisy. And bless the food." He shuddered a deep breath. And then looked dubiously at his plate. "Is that all?"

"Is what all?" asked Faith.

"Your dinner? Is this all you had?"

"We don't mind potatoes. Like them mashed," said Philip pulling his mother's half uneaten plate in front of him and helping himself to her cold leftovers.

"But did you have meat, or something else?"

"Nope," said Philip.

"Just potatoes?"

Faith looked impatient that he was unwilling to understand. "I can't do the hot water by myself, but I can show you where Mum keeps the tealeaves... and sugar... for visitors."

He nodded and got up to pour the hot water from the kettle.

The frown on his forehead had not eased when he pulled the cart up outside the town's infirmary. He jumped down and lifted both Faith and Philip down.

"Is little Daisy going to be okay? What's wrong with her?" asked Faith as she tucked her hand in Mr Galloway's as they walked up the path.

"I don't know," he said evasively, and he looked shocked at her little hand that she placed confidently in his. "We will see what Doc Mortimer says."

When he opened the door, Flynn glanced about the room with a frown. He did not see Sal sitting in a chair feeding Daisy quietly behind the screen. The Doctor looked at the children over his round rimmed spectacles and said, "Sister Blaine has some oatmeal biscuits out the back. Want to go and see her about that?"

Without any further encouragement Philip and Faith left in pursuit of the promised biscuits. Flynn raised his brow. Doc Mortimer was one of the Lenwick's oldest landmarks; his routine greeting was a frown and a dose of tonic rather than sweets. Perhaps this uncharacteristic leniency meant the news was not good. "Is she going to be okay Doc?"

"She will be. She is dehydrated. Cow's milk is not suitable for her."

"But she is a baby."

"Flynn, you baffle me. You are by yourself; you have a competent mother here who is willing to take care of your baby. Why would you not let Mrs Frazer nurse your daughter?"

"She said she would have to move in. I'm not ready for something like that. My wife is not yet cold in her grave."

Salome spoke from behind the screen. "Doctor, you know I have held to my rule of only one baby at a time. I have my own children to consider. But if I do this, I will do it in a way that is best for Daisy," said Sal definitely. "That means I need to be available. In the home."

Flynn blinked and stammered. "But..."

"But nothing!" Sal continued from behind the screen. "Believe me, I am genuine when I say that I have not the slightest inkling to pursue the idea of making this a permanent arrangement. I cannot... I will *not*... expose my children to your inconsiderate rudeness indefinitely. What I do is for a season, but I will not marry you!"

The doctor sat down and sighed. "I need you both to consider what is important here. I will be frank: the thing that is urgent right now is this baby. Whatever disagreements you have, you need to set them aside for Daisy so that she gets the care she needs."

"I have always been willing to care for Daisy," said Sal from behind the screen, a harsh defensive edge in her voice.

"You are using her as leverage to pursue your own agenda. That is not showing any concern for her situation, nor mine! It is..."

"That's ridiculous! It was just a way to make it work. I never suggested..."

The doctor whistled through his teeth. Daisy cried. "Grief! You might not be planning to tie the knot, but you are behaving like an old married couple. Now set aside whatever personal differences you have and look after this baby!"

"Doc, just find me another wet-nurse."

"There is no other nurse."

"What about the one over by the schoolhouse... Smith... Smythe...?"

"Mrs Smythe already has four other children she is caring for, her own six besides, with another on the way. There is not enough room for another baby. If you think you can talk someone else into it, you are welcome to try. Mrs Holmes has not long had a baby. She might consi..."

"The undertaker's wife? Greif! You can't be serious! He has just put my wife in the ground!"

"Regardless, right now, this baby cannot have cow's milk, and here is a nurse willing to give her care. It makes no sense that you are so dogged about this."

Flynn went quiet.

Doc Mortimer stood up. "I will go and give the children their tonic... and a check-up." He left the room.

Flynn poked his head around the screen. Salome sat there feeding Daisy. He swallowed and diverted his eyes, shaking his head. His wife was supposed to be doing this.

She looked at him. "This is just about Daisy, remember."

"Will you do it then? Look after her?" he said, gazing at the cornice on the ceiling. He frowned and swallowed hard as he remembered how his wife had painted and set up the nursery. She had been so excited.

"Of course. I told you that. But you also know what I need so I can do this. My circumstances have not changed. Otherwise, I will be out on the street. I won't be in a position to look after my own children, much less Daisy, or anyone else in the future. I need your help Flynn Galloway, and you need mine. It's not ideal. I get it."

He took a deep breath and said nothing for a long time. "Okay then. You said a year. I didn't think it was that long... you know... that they needed... well before they were able to eat normal food."

"Of course. But it is still usual for them to have some milk. I really do need a year, and that is more or less when I weaned Faith. I fed Philip for much longer. As I said before, once Daisy turns one – I will leave. If the matter is manageable earlier, you can find someone else to look after your animals. Daisy can come and stay with us in town while you are away at the camp if you need her to. That way you will have your home back."

"Let's just focus on what is immediate. Give me your papers tonight and I will look them over. If it is as you say, we'll make a plan. But this is all in the service of caring for Daisy. Just like the doctor said."

Salome looked down at the baby asleep in her arms. "Well, at least that is something we agree on. I can't think of a better reason to make this work..." she said with a soft smile.

* * *

6.

Sal woke with hope turning over in her belly. Today, a plan to regain her footing was being made. Flynn arrived early on his saddle horse, smartly dressed in his town shirt. He sat stiffly at the table while the children ate boiled eggs and dipped their toast fingers into the runny yolks. He watched Philip using his toast as a toothbrush making more mess over his face and shirt than Flynn ever conceived was possible. Philip looked up and saw Flynn watching him. "Do you want one? I can share."

Flynn gagged and looked away. "No thanks. Your mother is making me a cup of tea."

"I am? Oh yes. Of course, I am." Sal quickly poured hot water into the teapot and set it in front of him to draw.

"Milk?" he said staring that the chaos covering the table.

"I only have breast milk this morning... so you will have to forgo that treat."

Flynn frowned. Milk was not a treat. It was necessary for cups of tea... and children... but not babies of course – he realised that now. In a swirl of toast crusts, and eggshells, and face-washers, the kids were released out to the yard to play while Sal settled at the table to talk to Flynn. She scraped away some mess to make some space.

"So, Mr Galloway, did you look at the papers I gave you?"

"I did."

"And...? Will you help me? So, I can help you with Daisy?"

He sighed. The expression on his face told the story that he could well have gone to the chemist shop have his teeth pulled this morning. mThe druggist had a chair out the back for that. He would rather have been anywhere else. "Yes. I will."

"Oh, thank you Mr Galloway. Thank you!"

"We will go and satisfy the loan this morning. You can move your stuff in while I am away." He looked around and sighed. "Then when I get back, we will see what is needed to make this rentable." He was resolved, definite and cold. Desperation had a way of prising open doors.

"Oh." She blinked. She had prepared herself for more cajoling. "You don't have to pay the lot... just..."

"That will be cleaner. Banks are failing... and to be honest I don't trust them. These are uncertain times. And it will also mean less time you need to stay out at home."

"If you do this, you will not own me Flynn Galloway."

He shrugged. "I think I will. On paper at least." He took a drink of his tea and thought that life could not get worse than being a widower, with a newborn, and an obligation to try and find a way to make life work now.

Sal changed her dress, fed Daisy and made the kids pack a play kit to take next door to Mrs Trimboli, who had offered to look after them while this business at the bank was attended to. Philip was planning to dig her potato patch, more with the hope of finding grubs and worms than pulling weeds. Faith was going to help Mrs Trimboli cook. Sal had the fleeting thought that Flynn, dressed in his town clothes, did not look at all like an exhausted timber getter, or the broken widower, or the father of a young baby who stretched him beyond his resources.

He looked her up and down and sighed. "Don't you want to put on a town dress?"

"Actually, this is my church dress."

"Oh. Well. Let's get this over with then."

He pulled the buggy up outside the bank, he went around to the passenger side and offered Sal his hand. There was no hint in his demeanour that he resented this arrangement, nor that his daughter was his only motivation. She felt herself rise to his lead. There would be no hint on her part either that she was a desperate widow or that his daughter was her ticket to independence. She allowed him to open the door to the bank, and to hold the chair as she sat.

Flynn spoke decisively, without embellishment. The manager raised his brow. "Are you two getting hitched then? This palaver wouldn't be necessary if we just had the marriage certificate."

Flynn did not blink. "Mr Symanski, I don't want to give the impression that I am keeping company with a widow as a way to access her material assets. No gentleman would do that. We settle this first."

Sal inhaled quickly and took out her handkerchief to cover her disgust.

Mr Symanski raised his bushy brow and looked at Flynn with a smirk. The heavy sarcasm that would suggest this poverty-stricken woman had dowry was disconcerting... even for him. There was only one 'material asset' that she obviously had to offer. He caught sight of the cold, calculated light in Flynn's eye, and coughed uncomfortably. Regardless, their private arrangement was no business of his, and he was grateful to clear his desk of this headache. He rubbed his chest with his fist over his heartburn and quickly finalised the documents. He'd seen too much to know small matters like this, those that involve widows and children, just ruin a reputation, and annoy the bosses upstairs. He had bigger problems to be sure. He pushed the documents over to be signed and Flynn shook his hand.

Flynn opened the bank door and Salome walked past him without any acknowledgment. She climbed into the buggy, staring down the street with a frown. "Keeping company? Why would you say that?"

"Whether you like it or not, Mrs Salome Ivy Frazer, I am now your financier, and you are coming to live in my home."

"You gave him the impression that we are a couple. Or at least considering it."

"This community is going to make some assumptions about what we are doing, and their conclusions will be less than honourable. This decision impacts, not only your reputation, but mine. If it wasn't for Daisy, there is no possible reason I would proceed with this. But you have made a point. We need each other. I even thought about getting rid of my animals, so it was less complicated. But you need the rent from your place, and the reality is that my animals keep me sane. So, the animals stay, and that means I need the ongoing services of a caretaker. Regardless of how we view this arrangement, I am — in their eyes, a desperate man unable to manage without a wife. You are now a loose woman, without a ring on her finger, living in sin, selling your body for the comfort of a bed and a nice house."

Sal blushed bright red. "You bastard!" she muttered under her breath.

Flynn started the engine, and it spluttered. He turned towards her unperturbed. "I was not the one who suggested this tawdry arrangement. I have resisted it right from the start. But since we are here... we will make the best of the next twelve months. And then you can go back to your little hovel, looking after other people's babies. It remains to be seen if you will be able to pick up the remnants of your respectability after this. And I will get on with my life, raising my daughter... alone no doubt. Because I am pretty sure, no woman worth her salt, will look twice at me now."

* * *

7

Packing up and moving her things out to the farm was a massive endeavour by herself. Flynn's unsanitized summary of their arrangement took any gloss off her plan for independence. But this was not the first time she had pushed through with a plan that was not exactly her dream. Her marriage to Pedro was one of those things.

Sal paced herself by tackling one room in her house each day. Then she moved those boxes out to the farm in the afternoon when she attended to the chores. Mrs Trimboli continued to look after the children, including little Daisy during the day, giving her a bottle of expressed milk, so that Sal could get most of the cleaning completed. Mrs Trimboli organised for her sons to build a chicken coop in her backyard. They arrived with their tools and their kids, and a stack of salvaged and repurposed materials. The henhouse appeared behind her garden shed, near the outhouse, in an afternoon. The abundance of people and food gave the occasion the feel of a traditional barn-raising. That diversion had Philip and Faith entranced for hours.

By the end of the week Salome's little cottage was vacated. She unbolted the wooden bed frames and Mrs Trimboli's family helped load their truck with the last of her things. Philip took on the job of transferring the chooks to the new coop next door with great seriousness, catching each one in a flurry of feathers. The chooks were at last happily relocated into their new home for a temporary twelve months. The scale of this endeavour was like moving to the moon, rather than to the edge of town, even when she left most of her furniture behind. They agreed to visit Mrs Trimboli every Sunday after church so they would not lose contact completely.

* * *

Salome stacked her boxes on the verandah. Mrs Trimboli enlisted one of her sons to help reassemble the beds. The room which had been a home office space, was emptied for their use, and Flynn moved the desk into his bedroom. It was now occupied with two bunks for Phillip and Faith. The third bunk went into the nursery beside the cot. At least they all had a place to sleep. The rest they could work out when Flynn returned.

Within a few days they recaptured their previous rhythms of living on the farm. They resumed the routines of milking the cow and feeding the goat and the pig and collecting the eggs. They were laughing over dinner about some of their adventures when Flynn came in the door, tired from his shift rotation at the camp. "I see you made it out here well enough," he said civilly, as their chatter suddenly collapsed into silence.

"Ahh yes. We have conquered mountains other people flinch at climbing. I will clear the boxes from the verandah... just wanted to check where I can put them first. Right now, you need food. If you wash up, I will heat your dinner."

He went to the bedroom expecting to see the same rough and tumble invasion that confronted him last time. Instead, his bed was neatly made with clean sheets, the washstand was free of any clutter, and a fresh towel hung on the washstand rail. After he washed up, he sat on the bed in a slump. God give him strength. He braced himself with a deep breath and went out to the table. After he bowed his head to say grace, Sal stood up and handed Daisy over to him without even asking, and then served his meal, of salted meat and vegetables.

43

He sat awkwardly, holding her like a prickly bundle of barbed wire. He quickly handed Daisy back when his plate arrived. "Not just potatoes tonight then?" he said with raised brow.

"You have a well-stocked garden and pantry. You will have to tell me Joy's planting cycle, so I can keep it going. I never bothered at home because Mrs Trimboli' garden was always so generous."

He jolted and stayed focused on his plate. "Then why a meal of just potatoes?"

"Well, you know... sometimes the produce needs to be sold rather than eaten. But we were always offered the seconds, the marked or bruised produce tastes just as good when it is cooked."

As Flynn tucked into his meal, Philip's eyes did not leave his face. "Are you our father now?" he asked soberly.

Flynn gagged, and swallowed, and froze.

"Philip, we talked about this. Mr Galloway is helping us, and we are helping him by looking after Daisy and the animals. We are just family friends helping each other out. But at the end of the year, when Daisy has her birthday, we will be moving back home."

"But I like it here. I want to stay."

"I know honey. It is lovely. But Mr Galloway is not used to having so many people around, and it will be good for him to settle back into his own routines once Daisy is old enough. After we return home, she can come and visit at our house while Mr Galloway is away."

"So, we get to keep the baby?" he asked with relief.

"No. Daisy is Mr Galloway's daughter. We are helping by looking after her. But we cannot keep her."

"But I love little Daisy Hope. That's not fair."

"Yes, I love her too Phillip. Loving her does not change. We will always love her. Remember how we loved the others who came to us for help as well?"

"I didn't like them Carson kids. They were mean."

"Think how big our family would be if we kept all the ones we did like."

"But this is different. I want to keep *her!*"

"I know honey... and right now we can pretend. We can pretend we are all Daisy's family... and then, when we move back home, we will remember that she needs to stay with Mr Galloway, and she will always be our special friend."

Flynn said nothing during this exchange. He stared at the turnips and steamed marrow on his plate and watched the freshly churned butter melt through his spinach. Salome diverted the conversation to the current clucky chook situation and their adventures of feeding Pork Steaks.

After dinner, and stories, and prayers, and bed, Salome came out and sat at the table where Flynn still presided over his teapot. He pointed to it. "Do you want a cup of tea?" He had collected a fresh cup from the china cabinet.

"I usually keep tea for visitors."

"Hmm, I know. Perhaps if I was a drinking man, I would go for something stronger, but tea seems an appropriate choice to acknowledge the start of this arrangement." He poured her a cup while he said it.

"Oh okay. It still seems unnecessary... given I am not a visitor now."

"Or... we can say you are... on extended visitation."

"That sounds like calling on someone in prison. Incarceration is not exactly what I had in mind."

"Not an unsuitable comparison," he muttered. He took a breath and shrugged. What you said before... explaining all that to Philip – I thought you handled that well. What he said freaked me out a bit."

"Well, I have come to learn that kids in general, and Philip in particular, are pretty good at saying it exactly how it is. And I have learnt it is best to respond with equal candour, without trying to skirt around the issue. It is easier that way."

"Hmm. Nothing about this is easy."

"Well Flynn, you have gone from being a honeymooner, to having your house overrun by a ready-made family."

"We were married for seven years."

"Yes, and that sort of change takes a great deal of adjustment. This sudden tidal-wave of family must be tough. But I want us being here to be helpful... not just a painful reminder of what you and Joy have lost."

"Greif. I can see where Philip gets his ruthlessly honest tendencies from. No one, and I mean no one at all – not even Reverend Mason, talks about her like you do."

"Do you want me to pretend that Joy is not Daisy's mother? She is a very important part of her life, and her story. Surely you don't prefer that I never mention her at all?"

He took a swallow of tea. "I guess not. It is just hard to hear her name like that."

She nodded. "I felt the same way when Pedro died. No one would talk about him, and I felt that in some way he had become a shameful secret. But regardless of what our relationship was like, I want the kids to know about their father."

"What do you mean? What was your relationship like?"

"Well... it started out well enough I guess... but as things got tougher, Pedro took up gambling and in the end was as lazy as a lizard sunning himself in winter. He managed to whittle away just about everything we had. Even the motorcar. But I would not let him get hold of the house. I held on tight to that, right until the end. But then he got sick, and as idiotic as it sounds, I felt an obligation to fight for him. The truth is... part of me didn't want to. Still, it seemed like the right thing to do for the kids... so I could say with a clear conscience that we tried everything. I was angry for a long time that the battles I had fought to keep my home secure, were for nothing. It was taken by him in the end anyway. We had so many arguments about that house."

"Ahh. Hence why you are still fighting to keep it."

"That... and having a roof over my head. I know, as far as real estate goes, it is unimpressive, but it is a home for my family, and that means more to me than the actual rickety old shack itself."

"Then Mrs Frazer... I promise not to gamble with your inheritance."

* * *

They went through Sal's house the next day, making a list of things that could not be put off... and then they added to the list, many other things that should be sorted quickly to get it to a rentable state. Flynn knocked on a few of the walls as he looked around. "These timbers are solid. Despite how it looks, this house has good bones. It will do up well enough."

The top of the list was to fix the sag in the living room floor by leveling the house stumps. And the corresponding sag in the roof, that leaked when it rained as well as the guttering that was clogged and falling off. Then there was a smashed window boarded over; some broken shutters; a wobbly step; and a hole in the fence.

Sal blushed at the list. "It really is a lot. Leveling requires a builder, and the new tenants have a dog, so the fence can't be postponed either."

"We will do it ourselves," was all he said. Flynn disappeared in his cart and returned with a toolbox, jacks and plenty of timber of various lengths and widths, a string line, and a water leveling tube. Salome looked at the collection. "So do you need me to help with this?"

"I do. See if Mrs Trimboli will take the kids. They can come and fetch you when Daisy needs a feed."

They crawled under the house to begin working on the problem. Flynn stopped and put down his tape after the sixth question and bumped his head on a bearer. He swore and rubbed his scalp. "I can't spend all day answering your questions. I need to be able to do this without a full inquisition. You look after my daughter without an interrogation every time she burps, so just follow my lead, and our time will be more productive."

"But why do you..."

"Na-huh." He moved and cracked his head again. "Just save your questions until we have a comfortable seat and a cup of tea."

Flynn found the lowest stump and marked an 'X' with chalk. Then the highest stump was marked, and using the water level, they ran string lines like a criss-cross web between the piers. They measured what was needed to make them uniform heights and started to jack and lift and insert wedges and levelling-blocks, all the way around. They emerged covered in dust, cobwebs and grime, had lunch, then went back under. In the late afternoon they called it a day.

They bundled the kids onto the back of the cart and made their way home. As they pulled up Flynn said, "Philip and I will do the animals, if you want to take a bath and start dinner."

Salome drew the bath, washed the baby, and went to pull some turnips, while Faith had her bath. As she started the fried vegetables and salted beef, her thumping and banging became louder and louder. By the time Flynn came inside with Philip, Faith was quietly setting the table and keeping her distance from where her mother was whacking things around the kitchen. Sal firmly directed Philip to the tub while she continued to prepare dinner. Then Flynn took his bath, and they all sat silently at the table while the percussion continued. Just as the plates were set down, Daisy began to stir, so Sal went and attended to her. By the time she returned, the other two were tucked in bed. Flynn had been given directions on which book he was to read and which prayer he was to say, and Sal finally got her bath. Eventually she sat down at the table to eat her dinner.

Flynn cleared his throat. "I'm taking my cue from one very frank four-year-old, and I will try to be straight-forward. Right now, I am very confused. I thought we had a fair crack at what we had to get through today. I know we didn't get it all done, but we made good progress. It is a big job. There is no possible way we could have finished it all today." He poured her a cup of tea and pushed it towards her.

"I know."

"I'll answer those questions you had now, if that is what this is about."

Sal stared at him over the rim of her cup. "I am not upset."

"You may not think so, but my chopping board and cleaver would disagree."

"Disagree? Humph! Exactly!"

"What... exactly?"

"We didn't disagree – we didn't fight... or argue... not once! I get more consideration from someone who despises and holds me in contempt, than I ever did from my husband who was mandated to love and protect me. It makes no sense to me! None whatsoever! How is that even possible?"

"I don't dislike you."

"Of course you do. You have been very clear about the disgrace you are subjected to... by having someone in your house who is *selling herself* for a living. I believe that was how you put it."

"I..." His mind went blank. He poured himself another cup of tea to stall and gather his thoughts. "I meant that is how other people will interpret our arrangement. I don't think that. And I don't dislike you," he repeated.

She stared at him, and there was nothing in his look that suggested that he was not sincere. She grunted again. "Humph! Well, I still don't get it. And I'm not discouraged by our lack of progress. I am actually excited by what we achieved. I have waited a very long time to have these jobs attended to."

If this was her being excited, Flynn wondered what agitation might look like. "So, no questions then?"

"Not really... I didn't understand what you were doing to start with. Never seen anyone do that before. But it felt... coherent... the way we worked together. Like we made sense. Still... it is a little weird, since I've never experienced that. Gives me hope this arrangement might actually work though. How long do you think it will be until a tenant can move in?"

In some way, that honesty helped to establish the lines between them. They set about the business of working through the plan to get as much finished as they could, before Flynn went back to camp.

* * *

8.

Sal finally agreed that Flynn would go with her to sign the new tenants on. "I'm protecting my investment," he said when she insisted it was unnecessary. He eyed the scrapy yard, and the holes dug around the step by the dogs that yapped at him when they came in the gate. There were bones and broken bits of furniture and various layers of rubbish scattered about.

Flynn greeted Silas Carson – the man of the house, who didn't bother to stir himself out of the squatter's chair on the verandah. Silas bellowed at a posse of kids that came careering around the corner of the house, tempers hot and old shoes flying. "Oi! Settle down there you little stinkers. Can't you see we got visitors?" He was greeted with a volley of accusations justifying their vicious pursuit of justice.

"We will need the name of your current landlord to get a reference," Flynn said without hesitation.

Silas grunted. "The woman said we had the house – no questions asked. Since we're going to a cheaper place, it strikes me it's got be a dump. It's even cheaper than this... and this place *is* a dump. Don't need to get all official over a dump."

For someone who had been quite disparaging about Sal's house, Flynn hardly noticed that he was now protective of her little 'dump'. He had nailed and levelled, repaired and replaced, scrubbed and painted. Now it was a respectable little cottage. "We will let you know if your application has been successful Silas," he said as he turned around and walked out the gate.

Sal stared at him confused as they sat back in the cart. "I found these tenants. I used to look after a couple of their kids when Mrs Sams... Never mind. You can't just come in and take over like a bull charging all over the place. You told them they have to apply! I was supposed to sign them on today. I need them."

"No, I don't think you do. I didn't work like a slave to have them trash your house within the first week. We can do better. I'm going to talk to Reverend Mason."

Salome caught up with Mrs Trimboli while he did that. Mrs Trimboli fussed over how she had missed them all very much and that she was probably going to die before her time from loneliness. Salome nodded sympathetically and turned away to shield her smile. Mrs Trimboli might not be tall, but she had a large way of speaking from her large heart. She always had room for one more... even when her grandchildren were with her constantly. Mrs Trimboli made some cutizza – an Italian dessert that resembled large pikelets. When Sal called them pikelets for ease, she was always corrected. "I will make an Italian out of you yet, *mia cara*." Mrs Trimboli told the kids again what a blessing the steady supply of fresh eggs from their chickens had been. They sat up at the table with clean hands, smearing fresh honey with sticky fingers all over their warm cutizza. Then Mrs Trimboli filled a box with some homemade mulberry jam and a bottle of honey from her son's beehives, and a selection of fresh tomatoes and onions from her garden.

* * *

"Mr Galloway, I need to ask you about the nature of your relationship with Mrs Frazer."

"Excuse me Reverend, but I cannot see how that is relevant to whether you know of a respectable family. These times are hard; you must know someone who needs an affordable house."

"Well, Mr Galloway, the key word here is respectable. I cannot have you tenanting houses out when your own living arrangement exposes your daughter to ungodly and unchristian behaviour in the most licentious way."

"Hmm. You do know that Mrs Frazer is the nurse? She has been looking after Daisy since my wife died. If you have doubts, you can confirm this with Doc Mortimer. He was at her birth. And Thomas Holmes – the undertaker."

"Yes, of course I know all that. I did conduct the funeral."

"Then what seems to be confusing? She is caring for my daughter."

"She is living *in* your house... under your roof."

"She is caretaking the place because I work *away*. A lot."

"But she stays there when you come home."

"Reverend, what is it you would like to know?"

"I need to know that the moral concerns of my parishioners are given every consideration. You have denied nothing."

"I came here for a recommendation for Mrs Frazer... someone who might rent her house... perhaps one of your parishioners."

"Well, given the circumstances, I don't think I know of anyone who would be suitable at all. Such an endorsement would be sanctioning your situation. You have no idea what sort of moral avalanche this could trigger."

"Well thank you for your frankness, Reverend. Mrs Frazer will see you on Sunday."

"I will see you too no doubt. You will be attending Sunday worship as usual of course."

"Actually, I will be going back to work. I have stayed this time, longer than *usual*." Flynn stood, his irritation getting the better of him.

"But previously you were able to return after the Sunday service."

"Previously I was not accused of being a shameless fornicator, living in sin with a harlot."

"Mr Galloway! Mind your tongue! I never gave voice to such an accusation! Yet you must be aware that even Jesus embraced the sinner without endorsing the sin."

"Hmm. Well Reverend, it seems we differ on how you choose to embrace this particular sinner."

"We all fall short of God's glory. However, it is incumbent of me to warn you Mr Galloway, that your salvation is on uncertain ground."

"Then I am grateful Reverend, that God is my judge and not your good self. Good day."

* * *

Flynn sat down at Mrs Trimboli's table as they poured him a cup of coffee, and he helped himself to the batch of fresh cutizzas. "Do we have a tenant?" asked Sal as she watched him pulverise his cutizza, spreading it too quickly with rhubarb jam. He said nothing. "Hmm. I'm going to guess he was not able to recommend a family."

"Hmm, he did not. The good Reverend could not offer a referral." He gulped his tea. "It seems our corruption is so contagious that he was obliged to protect his parishioners. A suitable tenant could not be identified."

Sal shook her head in disgust, went to say something, and then quickly stepped out to change Daisy's nappy instead.

Mrs Trimboli filled his cup again and poured one for herself and sat down.

"Well, Mrs Trimboli, it was predictable. The local parish gossip is in full swing. I'm sorry if your association with us will cause people to make assumptions about your own moral wellbeing."

"Pfft! There is not much I haven't seen or heard in this town. Whispering does not intimidate me. Besides, my son knows people. I will ask Marcello if knows of a family. You are right Mr Galloway: Salom-ee can do better than that Carson lot." Mrs Trimboli's drawling accent pronounced Salome's name with an extended "ee" sound at the end. It became even more pronounced when she was agitated. "Silas Carson is a brute, just like that husband of hers: a bully and a brute. Salom-ee put up with so much being married to that shirker. You see to it that Salom-ee does not put someone like him in there."

"Well, if your son knows of anyone, I would really appreciate the reference."

"And I appreciate you helping our Salom-ee like you do. I saw you working on that house, crawling in and out under that place... and all over the roof... and then scrubbing those walls and mending the window frames. It reminded me of the old times, when you were learning tools with my boys... how you came back and built your beautiful Joy her home. Never saw Pedro so much as lift a hammer the entire time he was there. They called him Pedro because he was short and dark, and they thought he had a Spanish way about him. He didn't have a drop of such blood or sense. No man I know, from any of the old countries, would treat his family like he did. All he did was shame the reputation of strong European men. Salom-ee says it was his sickness, but that is a like saying sunshine is a disease. It is not. It is the sun. Cards are not a sickness. They are cardboard. People are their own sickness..." Her voice had an intense edge to it, but then she sighed and relented. "I don't know...

perhaps it is true... people do get sunstroke. Who can say which really comes first? Was it really the chicken or the egg?"

* * *

There was a knock at the door. Sal quickly looked out the window and then opened the door. "Good afternoon, Reverend. Mrs Mason. How can I help you?"

"We have come for a pastoral visitation."

"Oh. Well, Flynn is away, and I am doing well enough." They stood there unmoved. They noted with grim frowns, her familiar use of Mr Galloway's name. "Umm... would you like to have a cup of tea since you have come all this way?" It was evident her visitors believed they had crossed oceans to get there. Bottlebrush Grove was considered to be far out in the country, even though it was expected the family would drive into town at any time of day or night. Sal stepped aside, as they walked briskly through the door.

Mrs Mason looked dubiously at the table where three rocks, a dragonfly corpse, a cicada's shell, a snakeskin, a praying mantis egg-case, and a jar of tadpoles had been added to the nature line-up. "Yes. Very well."

They drank their tea in silence. Mrs Mason tried a couple of times to make small talk, but it fell rather flat. Eventually she cleared her throat. "I will be taking the crocheted rug I brought over when the baby was born. Now that Daisy is older, there are other needful families who require it now. I pulled out many donated jumpers to make that blanket up."

Sal said nothing but retrieved the rug from Daisy's cot. She wordlessly folded it and place it beside her. Reverend Mason put down his cup. "Mrs Frazer, I must ask you to reconsider your living arrangements. You are putting yourself and your children at risk because of your wilful insistence

56

on being here. You are misusing the mercy of God as a license to live in this debaucherous relationship."

Sal almost laughed outright. Had they met Flynn Galloway? The man was a monk. Instead, she coughed it down into her kerchief. "Is that right Reverend?"

"Yes. It..."

"But doesn't scripture command us to look after widows and orphans?" she asked seriously.

"Of course, but..."

"Well, I am a widow – Mr Galloway is considering my situation. And Daisy is, in all respects, effectively an orphan... motherless all of the time, and fatherless most of the time... and I am looking after her. It seems to me we are fulfilling Scripture, not abandoning it."

"Mrs Frazer... Salome... I notice your name is a biblical one," he said soothingly.

"Well noted Reverend, but not a surprising observation given your profession. What is your point?"

"My point is that there are two Salomes in scripture. The first Salome was a harlot of a woman who danced before Herod and asked for the head of John the Baptist on a platter. The second Salome was the mother of John and James, the sons of Zebedee, disciples of our Lord. She was a godly woman who stood to comfort Christ and his mother at the cross."

"Fascinating..."

"Yes. What is pertinent is that both these women had a choice. One used her skills for evil... the other for ease and comfort."

"And what is exactly your point Reverend?"

"Do I have to spell it out?"

"Yes, I think so. I would be loath to misinterpret your intent here."

"My point is: which Salome would you like to be known for? The good or the bad? God hath given you skills, but I fear you are using them for evil!"

"Disturbing comparison. It does seem a weighty analogy to live up to."

"Young lady, I fear you are not taking this seriously. I am being most earnest."

Sal smiled. "Oh, I have no doubt of your earnestness Reverend. However, I will stay with my initial explanation of caring for widows and orphans. I understand that you are uncomfortable with our choices, but I am confident that God experiences no ill-ease on our behalf."

"How dare you belittle God's holiness and purity! You mock Him with your blasphemous tirade."

"That was never my intent." She stood up and handed the rug to Mrs Mason.

"So, you will continue to live here... in wilful rebellion?"

"Good day Reverend. Mrs Mason. Thank you for your visit, however, I must go... I have an orphan who needs my attention." Blissfully, Daisy cried on cue.

* * *

9.

Sal looked out the window and watched Flynn gently strolling around the farm at sunset with an elegant woman on his arm. She considered the smart travel suit and her fashionable high-heeled boots. At least some people escaped destitution during this all-pervasive Depression. It didn't seem right. Sal grinned openly as the lady sidestepped to avoid a puddle, and then in doing so stepped in a cow pat. Sal quickly moved away from the window as they walked up onto the verandah. When they came inside, Sal was sitting on the lounge bouncing Daisy on her knee.

"Salome, this is Louisa Rilston. She is staying with Mrs Trimboli for the next couple of days. We will be going out tonight, so no need to worry about dinner for us."

Sal stared for a moment at the visitor's pretty face and her elegant hairdo and then drew her attention back to Daisy. She stood up as she spoke. "Well, I trust you have a lovely time. Flynn, can I see you for a moment before you go?" She directed him outside onto the verandah, carrying Daisy on her hip.

He looked at the sprouting garden of poppies that Sal had planted near the steps. *Practical. No fuss.* That is what she had said. "You knew I would start dating again," he said quietly, with a sigh.

"Oh. Yes. Of course. I knew that."

"Louisa was a friend of Joy's. She was widowed after the stock crash."

"Oh. That is sad. Look, this is not about you dating. You do what you must do. But I did wonder if you realised that Moonshine is about to calf. Tonight. I've put her in the shed. I mention it because you seem... distracted."

"What? Now? You call my heifer Moonshine... and then she labours on the one *night* with a full moon when I have planned a date. Oh, that is not fair," he said with another sigh.

"In my limited experience, I have never heard anyone say farming has ever been fair." Sal grimaced with an amused shrug. "Philip thought the crescent on her forehead demanded that name," she said as she jiggled Daisy contentedly. "Faith thinks her milk will be highly sought after... like bootleg and moonshine. Regardless, there is no plot to disrupt your plans. Look, Spotty had no issues when she gave birth. I see no reason why you cannot continue on with your date undisturbed."

"I am already disturbed. And consequently, I need to be here. I'd better check her to see how she is going before we leave," he said with a frown.

"Well, I'll come with you, and you can tell me what to look for."

"I can easily cut dinner short if that is needed." They walked across to the animal shed together. The heifer was quietly labouring. "She's doing okay. I should be back in time," he said to Sal, as they were walking back to the house. He ran his hand restlessly along the neck of his heifer and massaged the back of his neck with his other hand and quietly cursed. "Maybe I should cancel..."

"How long have you been planning this?" she said as they made their way back to the house. Sal glanced up and saw Louisa staring at them through the window.

"The heifer... or the date?" he said.

"Well, I know about Moonshine. Had no idea you were keeping company."

"Months. Literally months. I am quite hopeful about this. Louisa didn't even blink when I explained that you were here."

"Well then, don't cancel. Go and have a nice time... and I'll see you in a couple of hours."

"If you are sure..." He reached out and caressed little Daisy, who smiled delightedly at her father.

"See, even Daisy agrees," and Sal laughed as the baby cooed and ahh and charmed her way even deeper into her heart.

* * *

Flynn pulled out the chair as they sat down at the café and placed their order from the menu board. Louisa had gone back the Mrs Trimboli's boarding house and changed her travel outfit. Her evening dress was flattering, even if it was not new. She looked over at another couple who were whispering behind their hands. "Am I being paranoid, or are we quite the centre of attention here?"

"We probably are, given that they haven't seen me out and about much since Joy passed. Louisa, thank you for coming. I know it hasn't been easy for you."

"More accurately, it's been a nightmare. I just wish I could talk to Joy. She would understand."

He nodded soberly. "Aren't we quite the pair."

Her husband Frank had been a shining star... until everything imploded with the stock market crash. The bottom fell out of everything. Her life, her marriage, her society friends, her home. Everything. It was too much for Frank. He was found by a colleague on the pavement when he came in early to clean out his desk. He was not the only one. But there was no sense of community rallying around in tragedy. This had been a lonely walk of shame. And the shame was not going away. Louisa had moved back to her parent's place and learnt to cover the humiliation, or to transfer it on to someone else.

"Oh. I thought the whispering might have been because of the Help. When you said you had a wet-nurse, I imagined some frumpy matronly middle-aged black woman."

"Louisa! If you don't mind... we don't talk like that here," he said with a frown. There was no doubt their outing would add fuel to the local gossip fire.

She raised her brow and lowered her voice. "I certainly did not expect an attractive young woman presiding over your home like she owns it."

"Look, she is still the nurse. Our relationship is purely professional."

"Is it really? Because what I saw, when you were walking back from the barn... I would not call that professional. Father has staff. He never carries on in such familiar way with any of them."

"Well, she is looking after my daughter. So, I guess we are friends as well." His frown deepened at that idea. He had never noticed the shift.

She scoffed. "Friends? Are you sure that is all it is? She has children of her own, who are living *in* your home. Don't they usually get someone else to look after their own spawn?"

Hmm. "Spawn? Oh. Right. The kids." Flynn looked at her soberly and twisted his mouth thoughtfully. "What exactly did they say to you?" he said, swallowing some of his drink. This should be good.

"Philip, is it? He made it sound like a job interview. He said you needed a wife to take care of your animals while you were away. He took ages to explain how to feed the pig swill and scraps. He showed me a hole in his pants the goat ate, because you can't afford mash. And then there was a detailed account of the goanna they caught red-handed in the chicken coop, which stole all their eggs, so they ate the goanna instead for breakfast!" She shuddered in revulsion.

"We didn't eat the goanna," Flynn said, his frown melting as he tried to keep a straight face. "But I've heard it tastes like chicken."

"That's disgusting."

"Only if you're not hungry."

"Regardless Flynn, I don't do animals. I don't even have a cat. And if I did, I certainly would not feed it myself. Much like babies. I wouldn't do that either."

"Oh?"

"And the girl... she asked how I liked the idea of living all alone out here, since they don't see anyone for weeks and weeks, until you come home. *And* she had a snake story... on the verandah."

"Hmm."

"Even Mrs Trimboli spoke about how your milkmaid is looking forward to relinquishing the care of your daughter when you remarry. I had assumed she would stay on as the nanny, and at the very least, you would have a farmhand to do the chores."

"She is not my maid, or farmhand. The only nanny we have is our goat named Spotty."

"And *then...*" She paused dramatically as if this final tale topped all the others. "Mrs Trimboli says she cooks a Sunday risotto, so there is at least one day a week when the woman has *"some adult conversation'*. The way she says '*Salomeee'...* it sounds more like peasant-sausage than someone's name. I suppose that is fitting. It is all very... let me say... ethnic, even if affable. Very un-English. Do you keep *any* company that is not... ethnic?"

"Oh. Well, apart from Sal, no... not much, actually. Not now-a-days..."

"Flynn, I agreed to come out here to see your home in the country, and to meet Joy's daughter... but the truth is, I had hoped you might move back to the city."

"I'm not moving back. This is the house I built for Joy. It is Daisy's home."

"Look, I do understand why Joy married you. She was more at ease in her parent's garden and her painting studio, than on the dance floor. Father respects your business sense and that is a genuine reference in my eyes. And although your daughter is a cute little button, I am not going to marry to become a farmer's wife... isolated away from all civilised society. They used to mistake Joy and I for sisters, but this? I am not like Joy at all."

"Well, that is... candid." Given Louisa's frankness, Flynn was surprised that her and Philip had not hit it off. He took a drink and noticed a weight lift from around his shoulders. "So, what are you going to do? I had a line-up of country hospitality planned for the next couple of days."

"Which would be all very nice I am sure... but I don't see the point." Their meals were served, and they started to eat. She picked at some of the vegetables and pushed a fair portion of her meal to the side of the plate, screwing up her nose. "I will be leaving tomorrow. I think that is best."

"Hmm. Well, since this evening is all the civilised company you will allow me, give me an update on the society page while we have dessert." He had ordered bread and butter pudding. "And then I have a heifer to get back to. Her first calf." He smiled benignly and comfortably drank his wine. This was for the best. Besides, she had called Daisy *'Button'*. Louisa was right: this would never work.

Louisa launched into the more comfortable topic of society. Flynn tried to stay with her, but he could feel his eyes glazing over and suppressed a yawn. Louisa put down her spoon. Before Louisa was married, she was used to considerably more distress when she turned suitors away. However, it was different now that she was a widow. Dating seemed more like thrashing out a business arrangement than courting. Perhaps her father was right, and it was about business-sense. She wished she could turn back the clock to when life was about attending dances and choosing hats for Race Week. "Are you angry that I have declined your overtures?"

"It would have been harder if we got further in... and then you told me you were out."

"Under different circumstances Mr Flynn Galloway, you would be quite the catch."

"Under different circumstances, I still could not see you being a farmer's wife. You were right to call it."

Louisa took a sip of her wine. "What did Nurse Sausage think about you calling on another woman?"

"Salome. Her name is Salome," he said patiently. "Well, she was worried about the heifer, but otherwise, she was very supportive... actually." He had merely assumed Sal would consider it inconvenient if this interfered with her timeline to save her home. He had been working on launching this relationship with Louisa for a while, and now he had to start at the beginning again. That was inconvenient.

"Supportive? That is an interesting way to view it."

"I hadn't mentioned you, so I think it was a bit of a shock for her to start with. Perhaps that was a little unfair, but it was agreed that at some point, I would start going out again."

"Yet you have not considered going on a date with her? She obviously meets the criteria of being able to handle the isolation, and your animals... and the snakes."

"I... ahh... I just never thought about it. I am more concerned that she looks after my daughter. That is all."

"Do you find her attractive? She is a pretty little thing... in a common, milkmaid sort of way."

"Oh. Like I said... just never thought about it."

She frowned. He surely was not being honest. "Well, Mr Galloway... I am surprised. Deny it all you like, but I think you should think about it. Because I am confident, given the look she tossed my way as we were leaving, that she has definitely given the idea a great deal of consideration herself."

* * *

Moonshine calved without assistance. The calf lay on the hay, moist and panting, and his young mother started to lick his dark coat.

"I wonder if it is because I am a mother myself, that I get excited about the arrival of the next generation," said Sal with amazement, as she watched the calf struggle to stand on her very wobbly legs.

"My experience on becoming a father wasn't great, so I just get nervous and jumpy. That's to be expected I guess," Flynn said as he added some fresh hay to the pen. He leaned on his pitchfork watching the calf struggle to his feet. It felt like he was learning to walk again too. He cleared his throat. "So, Sal, Louisa had to unexpectedly go back to the city, and I had a whole line up of country hospitality planned for the next couple of days. I really didn't want to waste the effort I gave to all the planning, so I wondered if we could do it together."

"Yeah, why not? It sounds like a bit of a distraction. The kids will love that, I'm sure."

"Oh. The whole family? Okay."

The next morning the kids stood up in the back of the cart as they went down to the creek. A throw quilt was spread on the grass and a collection of goodies from a wicker basket that Mrs Trimboli had prepared, was produced for a picnic. Sal had made an extra loaf of fresh bread for good measure, to go with their coveted jar of apricot jam, and one of her famous mulberry pies. The kids splashed in the shade of overhanging trees, building a dam with rocks and placed stepping-stones strategically across the creek. Faith made a water garden using duckweed and water reeds, bordered with smooth patterned river rocks. She commissioned Philip to catch guppies and tadpoles to populate this miniature home. It was relaxing and fun and a wonderful diversion from their usual routines.

"Thank you for inviting us along," said Salome as she packed away their lunch and the kids rushed back to splash in the creek once more before they went home. She positioned a couple of homemade toys on the rug in front of Daisy who happily ignored them and proceeded to chew on a stick peeled of its bark. "It's a shame that Mrs Rilston decided to forgo such a treat, but all the better for us. This has been lovely."

Flynn thoughtfully chewed on a blade of grass. Something was bothering him. "Louisa told me that Mrs Trimboli said you were looking forward to relinquishing care of Daisy. That shocked me. I thought you didn't mind doing this."

"Mind? I love Daisy! But I have to allow that it would be better for her to have a proper mother. She needs that. Still, like Philip said, if there was a way we could "keep her" ... I would do it in a heartbeat. So, I am not *looking forward* to it, as your Mrs Rilston suggested, Mr Galloway... but I do understand it is part of what we agreed to."

Flynn frowned and returned to a safer topic. His failed date. "I really thought Louisa might fit in here, but she made it crystal clear that this life was not to her taste."

"Where did you meet then? She doesn't look like the type to frequent timber-camps."

"In Sydney. She was a friend of Joy's. I was given a job by her father when one of his foremen was called away. That's how I met Joy... I was renovating their family loungeroom... more like a ballroom really."

"Renovating job? You worked as a builder?"

"Yes. How do you think I was able to fix up your house?"

"I thought you were a handyman... not an actual builder."

"You don't remember that I worked with Trimboli's?"

"A life with babies can be quite insular, I guess. I don't remember that."

"Louisa's father was the one who got me started in lumber full-time."

"*Got you started?* As in giving you a job?"

"Yes... her father's in construction. The industry has all but fallen over, but he is one of the few still left standing, so it is imperative I continue to work with him."

"Oh. I didn't know that." She paused and looked at him. "What exactly is your job Flynn Galloway?"

"What do you think it is?"

"You have talked about the timber-camps. I assumed you were part of a timber felling crew. You know... climbing trees like monkeys, using ropes and planks. Axes and saws. Or perhaps one of the crosscut crew down the timber pits. Probably with the standard role of the underdog... getting sawdust in your eyes and ears."

"Hmm. Not underdog. Top dog. I had more work supplying timber for other chippies than working on the tools myself. Most of what I do is management, contracts and keeping customers on board. Business takes me to the city on and off during the year. I don't spend all my time at the camps, but I've had to go out there more often while I'm training up a new crew-boss. I'm on recruit number five at the moment. With everyone looking for work I thought it would be pretty simple, but it hasn't been easy finding the right guy.

The fellow I have now was part of my crew in the city a while back. He's working out well."

"Oh. You *own* the business." Sal shook her head, stunned. "I am surprised by this."

"I put the crew together initially to stabilise timber supplies for my own jobs. Then others wanted that same sort of guarantee for supplies. Louisa's father signed my first major contract with me. The building boom took off and I had to throw everything at it to keep up. I was pushing for the day when I could ease off a bit. But after The Crash, most of my contracts disappeared overnight. I've struggled to keep my head above water. There are a lot of families depending on this work, so I can't pull back now. I have no idea how long we can keep going. I wish it had been different... so that I didn't need to be away so much. It must have been lonely for Joy waiting for me all the time. I truly regret that. I should have been here. She used to say that I could anticipate any sort of problem and proactively put solutions in place. But when it really mattered, I missed it completely. I didn't anticipate that she would not always be here."

"That's hard... ragged edges, when life isn't neat and tidy. It takes a particular kind of strength to acknowledge we missed important things. I admire your work ethic Flynn. Pedro never worked two days in a row with any consistency. I just never thought of you as a businessman."

"I've done my time in the sawpits – even as the underdog. Did you really think a labourer would have the where-with-all to put up your loans?"

"I just knew you had a job... when so many people don't. Probably a good thing I didn't know too much, or I would never have let you crawl around in the dust and cobwebs under my house. Makes sense though... how Joy was such a gentle-woman, and why you are setting your sights on the likes of Mrs

Rilston." There really was more to that statement when Flynn said she didn't have a chance with him. He must have thought she was a gold digger.

"So, you thought I was being too ambitious to ask Louisa out?"

"I thought that there was little chance she would fit in here. Without being too crass about it, Flynn, your Mrs Rilston is a snob. I cannot picture her feeding Pork Steaks household scraps."

He laughed. "She would refuse to even throw Rusty a bone, much less milk a cow. Yeah. It was never going to work."

She tilted her head. "I'm sorry. Are you heart-broken?"

"Probably. But not by Louisa. I was merely testing the water with her. Truth be known, I figured that if I could survive losing Joy, then anything else is not beyond me. Maybe even a Louisa."

"Well, her loss. She missed a perfect afternoon. Bottlebrush Grove definitely has the prettiest creek in the entire district."

Flynn laid back on the picnic rug and nibbled one of Mrs Trimboli's biscuits. He closed his eyes and considered something that he had not given a great deal of thought to before.

* * *

The next day they took a horse-riding excursion. Sal wrapped up Daisy in a shawl, slung tight against her body. To transform this outing into a family event, Flynn had some adjustments to make. His most placid ponies were given a solid workout and then they took the trail around the circuit of the farm. Flynn led them out past the boundary, up over the ridge to have a look at the sweeping views of Lenwick and the river winding through the valley. The kids pointed out the townhall clocktower, the church and the school. They even located their house next to Mrs Trimboli's. Philip insisted he could see their chooks. They had morning tea of oatmeal biscuits, before they wound their way home. Philip thought this extended horse ride was the best outing ever – the pinnacle of perfection! The next day there was a river boat excursion on the town weir.

As the children settled for the night, Sal sat at the table and smiled over her cup of tea. "You are quite the smooth host Mr Galloway. If Mrs Rilston had stayed, I doubt she could have resisted your charms as the country gentleman."

He chuckled. "What you see as charming, she saw as a plunge too deep to contemplate. I probably need to thank your kids for that insight."

Her eyes widened. "What do you mean? What happened?"

"While we went to check on Moonshine, they grilled Louisa about living in isolation, eating goannas, battling snakes, saving their wardrobe from being munched by Spotty and feeding our famed Pork Steaks swill. All the pressing obligations of a farming lifestyle," he said with an amused grin.

"They didn't! Oh Flynn, I am so sorry."

"It seems that their determination to sabotage my date was an act of mercy. I am not upset," he said with a shrug.

"Oh well, next time we will have to make a more watertight plan. I might be able to have the kids stay with Mrs Trimboli."

"There won't be a next time. Not with Louisa. Besides, you don't have to do that. This is their home while you are here. There is no need to hide them away."

"I just thought that you wanted this sorted before we leave. Having their scheming out of the way might be... well... helpful."

"Sal, have you ever thought about staying on?"

She frowned. "What? While you smooch your wife? Oh no. I don't think I'm up for that."

"No... I didn't mean... I just wondered if you had thought about staying on... if I didn't marry."

"Stay here? Forever? After you went to all that trouble of transforming my hovel of independence into a respectable cottage? No. I have not thought about that either."

"Oh." And he said nothing further as she got up to attend to Daisy for her night feed.

* * *

"Sal, I need to ask something. When Louisa was here, I became aware of something that I need to do. And I would like your help."

She looked up from where she was cutting salted beef and arranging it on sandwiches. She applied a very thin smear of pickles. Surely, he was not going to ask her to be a dating service... setting him up with local singles. "I guess you can always ask," she said cautiously.

"Well... I want to take Daisy to meet her grandmother. I haven't been able to face it until now. I think it is time."

"Joy's mother?"

"Yes."

"Oh. That's appropriate I guess."

"She lives in Sydney. Having Louisa visit, just reminded me what I have neglected. But I need you to come with us."

"You want me to go to *Sydney* with you?"

"Yes. I need you... to care for Daisy."

"Oh. The city?" Sal arranged the sandwiches on a plate, and wondered how she could avoid this. "Are you sure? What are we going to do with the animals and what about the kids?"

"We will work it out. Umm. There is something else."

"Oh?"

"I am going to clear out the Studio."

"Oh..."

"There are some paintings that I want to take back to her mother. There is that beautiful portrait that she did of her father. I think it is only fair."

"Oh... and the studio? What are you going to do with that?"

"I will turn it into my office. The space is just wasted the way it is. Things are settling down with the new foreman, and there are matters that I can attend to from home more easily if I have my office set up properly. The desk in my bedroom is not working well."

Sal smiled. The desk he referred to, was a huge monstrosity that he had snapped up for a bargain. The sale probably paid someone's rent for another month. It was jammed into the corner of his bedroom, taking up half the space.

"I might need your help... if you don't mind." There was no sense avoiding this any longer. He turned away, his face taking on that ashen shade of strain.

"Oh. Yes. Of course. Whatever you need." She paused as she felt the weight of what he had asked. "Flynn... I'll see if the kids can visit with Mrs Trimboli for the day... or longer if that is what you need. That way we can do what you need with privacy. I'll talk to her about going to Sydney as well."

He nodded. "I'm going out to check some fences. If you can get that sorted, we will start tomorrow."

How do you pack up, move on, clean out, without being disrespectful of what meant the world to you? Flynn sat out by the back fence under a tree, and he didn't move. He hadn't stepped inside her studio since that horrific night from hell. Sometimes he would accidently glance through the windows as he walked past the house and think he could see Joy standing at her easel or leaning over her table. Or at night, he would wake because he could hear her rummaging through her paints or dropping her brushes... and his heart would stop.

Somehow, he needed to say goodbye and this trip to Sydney was part of that. Besides Daisy needed to meet her grandmother. Sal was right: Joy's world was an important part of Daisy's story.

* * *

Flynn walked in the door later than usual and tripped over something in the dark. He lit the lamp and raised it in disbelief. He looked around in horror at clothes strewn across the floor and the general chaos that greeted him. It reminded him of the very first time he met this family... only worse, and he could feel himself start to steam. The kitchen was in disarray. There was a bowl of pancake batter beside the stove with crusty dribbles trailing over the frying pan and stovetop. He stood in the doorway to their bedroom. The floor was scattered with junk that Philip had collected and used as toys. Both Faith and Philip were asleep, but Sal's bed in the nursery was unoccupied. It could have been untouched for days if the layers of accumulated stuff were any indication.

He frowned and suspiciously went to his bedroom. No doubt Sal upgraded to roomier quarters. But when he opened the door, he was surprised. His room had been given an armistice to the anarchy that reigned everywhere else. His bed was made and undisturbed; the floor was clean; the washstand tidy. He turned around... and tripped over a towel that lay in the doorway. He swore under this breath and picked it up. Then he saw Sal propped on the lounge, dozing fitfully, nursing little Daisy at the breast. He went to take Daisy from her arms as she started to whimper... and he gasped. Even in the dim lamplight, he could see they were both covered in angry red spots. He raised the lamp; Daisy's tiny little face and body were a blotchy array of blisters. He stepped back and frowned and put down the lamp. He stood there watching them for a long time in a thoughtful gaze. Then he covered Sal with a light sheet and quietly went to the kitchen and started to tackle the mess.

He began to jigsaw an alternate story in his mind, as he scraped the plates and washed some dishes. He suspected this had been a marathon of trying to care for a very sick baby. His baby, while Sal struggled with being sick herself. Perhaps Faith had been trying to help by sorting dinner for her brother…. hence the batter disaster. He gasped and quickly grabbed the lamp, picked up the scrap bucket, and went out to check on the animals. He was not sure how they would have fared, if Sal had consumed every second caring for Daisy, when there was no one to care for her. The calf had been run with the cow, so who knows when they last had fresh milk. He locked the calf away and threw some hay into the yard. He checked the water troughs, which were low, but at least they still had water in them. He filled them up. Pork Steaks appeared to be the most neglected member of the household and enthusiastically gobbled the scraps thrown into her pen. He made up some mash for her and added that to her feeder.

When he came inside, he started clearing the things away from the walkways. He didn't do much; he was tired and went to bed. He stirred in the early hours of the morning to Daisy's frantic crying, and he could hear Salome pacing the floor… gently murmuring some sort of incoherent lullaby. He dragged himself awake and lit the lamp. He saw the look of worry on her face, distorted by the blisters around her brow, chin and neck. He came over to her, and she stepped back shaking her head.

"Oh Flynn, you are back. She is so hot. She is burning up again. I thought once the rash came that would be the worst of it… but this is just going on and on. This is much more serious than I supposed. You should stay away."

"I'm not going! You are sick yourself. You need help."

"I can manage. I am just tired. So tired..."

"Sal... look at your arms..." He directed her to the mirror behind the sideboard. She gasped as she saw the spotted mess that confronted her.

Flynn set the small metal tub they used to bath Daisy on the kitchen table, lit the fire and brought in jugs to fill it up. Sal directed him to add just enough hot water from the kettle to take off the chill. Sal undressed Daisy and put her in the water. She screamed and thrashed. Suddenly Daisy's body went stiff, and her eyes rolled back. Sal quickly pulled her out of the bath, her body jerking on the towel. "Please Flynn – please. Fetch Dr Mortimer or Sister Blaine. See if they will come. Oh Flynn, hurry. I am so sorry. So sorry. Please!" Tears streamed down her face. Daisy's little body went limp, and Sal wrapped her up loosely in a cotton shawl she used as a bunny-rug.

Flynn took Sal in her arms, and she leant hard on his chest as he held her, trembling with exhaustion. "Shh..." he said soothing her. "My kid-brother did that a couple of times as a baby when he had a fever. I remember being scared, but Mum insisted he'd be fine... he really was. I will go and see if I can get someone to come." He quickly left.

Sal held Daisy's hot little body was burning against her as she slumped in the chair. Everywhere they touched, their blisters hurt. Daisy irritably fought being held, but she also wanted to be comforted and soothed. Sal started to track around the room again, humming the little lullaby, as the baby whimpered and cried. It was just easier for Sal to hear her own crackling, tired voice, than Daisy's pained cries. She went back to the bath and tried to soothe her by floating her in the water.

Sal was feeding Daisy again, and dozing off, when she heard the door open, and Flynn came in with Sister Blaine. She looked about the room taking it in and then came over to the lounge where Daisy was feeding. She took the baby from her arms. Sister Blaine hesitated for a moment, and then she pressed her lips together and determinedly laid Daisy on the table, unwrapping her to check her over. She opened Daisy's mouth to check the blisters on her palate. Sal came and stood with her. Flynn hovered nearby. "What do you think Nurse?"

"She is a sick little girl. You said that she had a convulsion? How long did it last do you think?"

Sal shook her head... foggy from exhaustion. "I... I'm not sure..."

"Less than four seconds I reckon Nurse," said Flynn.

"Are you sure? It went on for a long time... it was much longer I think..." said Sal in a haze of worry and exhaustion.

"Well... keep an eye on it. If she's had one seizure, it is likely she can do it again. It happens when they get very hot. Try to keep her temperature down if you can. Sal, you are sick yourself. Baths for both of you are the best... which I see you have been doing for Daisy. Sweating it out until the fever breaks... that does not apply to little ones."

"Oh, this is terrible. Terrible! Will she die?" Sal felt herself unravelling.

"Sal, you have other children. Surely you have come across chickenpox before? Unless there is some complication, I am confident she will recover."

"Chickenpox? I was worried it might have been something more serious... like... like... we went to Sydney," she confessed in a rush. Her voice caught on a sob. Flynn put his hand on her shoulder as her body started to shake.

"Sydney? What do you mean? When did you go there?"

"Nearly a month ago... Sydney... I know they've had the smallpox there..."

"Oh. That Pox. The last smallpox outbreak in Sydney was over ten years ago and it was contained with quarantine and isolations. I, for one, am reassured that our health department takes an aggressive approach to public health and doesn't ignore these things. I know there has been opposition to the idea, but the new inoculations are working. There have been no new instances of smallpox for years. We are trained to look for it. In my assessment, I believe it is safe to say this is not a case of Smallpox. Besides, the incubation period for chickenpox is no longer than three weeks. I don't believe this is related to your trip to Sydney."

"But Daisy is so sick, and this is going on and on. I was sure it was something more serious..." Her brow was beading in sweat. Flynn sat her down and poured her a glass of water.

Sister Blaine nodded. "I agree that Daisy is a sick little girl but be reassured: this is not that sort of rash. This is chicken pox... but it is still serious none the less. Especially in children as young as Daisy."

"My other children haven't had it."

"Oh. Well..."

"Is this bad?" she said with panic rising in her voice again. "I know some mothers force their children to play with kids who have spots so that they catch it and get it over with... but I was never inclined. I kept them away."

"I am of the thought that wellness is always the better course. Intentionally exposing someone to sickness that cannot be predicted in its severity doesn't seem sensible to my mind."

"But I don't even know how she would have got it. Faith goes to school, but she has been well. We don't go out anywhere except to church on a Sunday. So many children play with Daisy in her pram..."

"Hmm... any of those could be the contact point. You probably will never know. They believe you catch the sickness even before there are any signs of it."

"Did I give it to her? I didn't have any signs when she started having fevers."

"Well, it doesn't really matter where she got it. Unfortunately, I can say with some certainty that I doubt your other children will escape this time. There is more to come. Have you had it?" she asked looking at Flynn. He nodded and she turned back to Sal. "Well, just keep on doing what you are doing."

"But I am not doing anything!"

"Sal, I know you are exhausted, but you are keeping her fluids up — and that is the most critical thing while they are running fevers. And you must drink extra yourself, or your milk will dry. The baths will help keep her cool. These blisters are not infected. I see how you have been swaddling her arms and hands, so she won't scratch. Perhaps try mittens as well, so that you can loosen her wraps and that may help keep her cooler. Both of you hop into an oatmeal bath together. That will help soothe the itch."

"Oatmeal?"

"I'll show Flynn how to prepare it. Just grind the oats to a powder in your mortar and pestle... nice and fine... then wrap it in a stocking, or even a cheese muslin... tie it up, and then soak the sack in the bath until the water goes a milky colour. Adding bi-carb soda to the bath water can soothe the itchiness as well... about half a cup. You can even make a paste out of the soda and the oatmeal, and paint the blisters, and see if that helps some. Other than that... it is just a matter of keep on keeping on."

When Sister Blaine left, they put Daisy back in the bath with the oatmeal pouch tied up in a handkerchief. The milky oat water did seem to offer some relief. "Sal... I'm here now. Have a bath yourself, then lie down. Don't disturb the others. You need sleep."

"But..."

"Yeah, don't worry. Just sleep."

She closed her eyes and felt like crying. "But Daisy..."

"I've got her. Remember what Sister Blaine said... there is more to come."

"I can't even think about that."

"Then lie down."

She looked at him gratefully. "Thank you..." She left. She didn't worry about the bath and just collapsed into a feverish sleep.

* * *

12

"Flynn is here!" yelled Philip as he flew out of the house to help him stable his horse. Flynn ruffled Philip's hair as he chatted by his side, filling in the details of what adventures had happened while he was away. Faith carefully adjusted some wildflowers that she had put in a jar on the table. Salome noticed a quiet release of tension in her shoulders now that he was back. She hadn't noticed that before.

When Flynn came inside, the house was orderly, and dinner was ready. That was a relief. It didn't look like a warzone ransacked by gangs of scoundrels. Tonight was calm. Good. That bode well. He smiled at Faith who discreetly came over and gave him a hug. Sal set Daisy down and she crawled over to him by the door. He reached down and picked her up. "Oh my! Look how fast you are moving now! How quickly you are growing up my pretty little Daisy!" He settled at the table. One of the chairs had a stack of books wrapped in newspaper and towels to boost Daisy's height so she could sit at the table to eat. He looked at the innovative construction curiously as Sal took her from his arms. "You could have told me Daisy needs a highchair."

"It does okay," Sal said dismissively as she tied a homemade sling to strapped her in, around the back of the carver chair. They said grace and Sal started to feed Daisy her mashed vegetables. Faith brought the other plates to the table. There was a splatter of pumpkin over Daisy's face, and they grinned at how clever she was. Then there were the usual night-time routines. Flynn pitched in and finally there was a quiet moment, while Sal gave Daisy her night feed. They sat in the lounge and chatted. This settling-in time, when Flynn returned from being away, was tricky. The usual rhythms they developed had to quickly readjust when he came home again. They found talking it out was one way to help the transition.

"So..." said Flynn, after they had talked for a while. "I was thinking I might try again."

"Try what again?"

"Try another date."

"Oh." Sal frowned and focused intently on Daisy sleeping in her arms.

"There is a lady I have met, and I have decided I would like to get to know her better... in a romantic way," Flynn said, watching her carefully.

"Oh? So, you are planning on bringing her out here? What would you like me to do?"

"Well, you suggested having the kids stay with Mrs Trimboli. I wasn't keen on that idea to start with, but you have made a good point, and I should know by now that what you suggest usually has some wisdom attached to it. Louisa made me very aware that this place can be a bit overwhelming. It has taken me a good many months to recover from her rather severe appraisal. I thought it might be helpful to create a bit of space. Of course, she must meet Daisy... so you'll be here. But rather than dining out, I thought a home-cooked meal would be pleasant. I am going to try and arrange this for the next time I am home... in three weeks. And since you are around, and we have that rather unfashionable role of a chaperone at our disposal, I thought she could stay... well, here... rather than in town. She could take Faith's bed... and."

"Chaperone? Huh. What's her name?"

"Irene. Ironically it is a name that also means Peace. You told me your name means that... when we first met."

Sal grinned. "And as I remember, you told me that was very odd. It seems to me Mr Galloway, that you are determined to have some Peace in your life, one way or another."

"You have no idea," he murmured to himself. He cleared his throat. "I, ahh... wanted your opinion. Of those activities I had planned for the lovely Louisa Rilston, which one do you think would appeal to a lady most?"

"Oh, the picnic for sure... down by the creek."

"Not the horse ride?"

"Well, if you were courting Philip, I would guarantee you'd be engaged before you rode out the gate! He loved it that much. But a lady may be less enthusiastic. And boating on the river was beautiful... but it does involve a little bit of mud and sludge getting in and out... and that potentially could spoil a moment, especially if your Irene has an inclination for fashionable boots like Louisa did. Or you could just spend some quality time feeding Pork Steaks scraps, or serving Spotty your clothes, and being upfront about your husbandry expectations in a spouse."

He grinned. "Clever. Husbandry. I fear my chances are not great. Still, I am determined to give this a try, as this particular lady is quite exceptional. Besides, this time we don't have any cows about to calve, so this may work in my favour."

"Your chances are fine, Mr Galloway. There is someone who will be the right person for you, I am sure."

"What about you? Is there someone for you?"

"Me? Goodness, no! Who is going to be enamoured with a woman who already has two kids, and insists on caring for other people's babies? I know I will not be able to do this forever... but it is something of a privilege for me. I always wanted a large family, but that never happened so this has helped satisfy my maternal nurturing. But I don't expect any man to understand that."

"So, it is not that you are not open to the idea of a husband... it is just that you don't believe anyone would be interested?"

"One thing Pedro did manage to provide, was a large dose of realism, and an equally large dose of sceptical pragmatism. You had Joy... a wife who loved and doted on you with stars in her eyes, so I understand that you would have a more open and optimistic view of marriage than myself. I have never had any reason to think that would be my lot."

"But what if, umm... if what you said is true, perhaps it also applies to you? You are confident there is a person for me. What if there was a right someone for you as well?"

"Huh. That would be a miracle... since I don't go anywhere to meet singles, and I don't have the time to give it any attention. These things don't just happen. They have to be nurtured... like your little Daisy."

"Well, if you help me with my quest... perhaps I can help you with yours."

"That's ridiculous. I still won't be able to meet, greet or give any relationship that sort of attention. My children are the love of my life now. I am content."

"You forget that I work in an industry where I come across a lot of single men. My overseer is an exceptional young man. Amiable... hardworking... good looking..."

"Ah no, thank you. No matchmaking. You just look after yourself, and I will be fine. Perhaps this Irene is the person for you."

He smiled and she noticed his eyes go soft as he thought about her. "Perhaps," he said.

She blushed and quickly stood up to settle Daisy in her crib. She didn't know this Irene, but she already didn't like her.

* * *

Sal went outside and paced up and down. Grief. It was absurd that she was getting upset. This was the plan. This was *always* the plan. But suddenly it seemed that her time at Bottlebrush Grove was drawing to a close far too quickly. Why couldn't Daisy stay six months old... eight months old, forever... needing her? Flynn needing her? Like when they went to Sydney. That trip was so hard for him, and she was there helping him through it. But that was over, and already time was marching on. It was wrong that Daisy's birthday, was looming on the calendar like a death knoll. It should be a time of anticipating celebration and excitement. Every time she thought about it, she dreaded the idea that Daisy's birthday marked the end of something wonderful.

Flynn's talk of Irene suddenly disrupted a contented feeling that had settled over her since the chickenpox nightmare. The kids had gone down like dominos. Sal sighed and shook her head. Of course they couldn't catch it all at once. Perhaps, because it had been such a difficult time, once she got to the other side of that episode, she felt more relaxed, more satisfied. Flynn had seemed more comfortable too, or at least she had thought so.

"Hey?"

Sal spun around and rubbed her forehead. "Hey."

"Are you okay? You seem... troubled. Is everything alright?"

"No... yes. No, I mean nothing is amiss. I'm okay. I just..."

"Just...?"

"Well, I was thinking about Irene coming. I think you really should get Daisy that highchair. You don't want to give the impression that you are skimping on your daughter's needs. That will not reassure a lady of your capacity for devotion."

"Oh. Have I been neglecting my daughter?"

She paused at the look of horror that passed over his face and then shook her head. "No of course not! You are a devoted father. Although I do remember a time when you were terrified of holding her. A little girl could not ask for a better father. I know that... but your Irene may be less convinced. You don't want to give her grounds for considering that you are a man who neglects those close to him."

"Oh. Yes. Good point. I believe you are absolutely right. I do not. A highchair it is. Is there anything else that may help make the right impression?"

"Oh, you know..."

"Salome, I have absolutely no idea. If I missed a highchair, which is obvious now that I think about it, what else is there?"

"Well, I have dressed Daisy in hand-me-downs that I have used for the other babies. A new outfit might be fitting for a special visitor."

"Oh. I did not even think about clothes. But this is an excellent point. We will have new outfits. That should be reassuring for the lady. We will go into town tomorrow and sort this immediately. And shoes."

"Daisy is still crawling... she doesn't really need shoes yet."

"I assume she will not always crawl, and she is walking around furniture, so consider it a pre-emptive gesture. I will need your advice on the highchair, and the clothes, so we will make an outing out of it. There was another activity of country hospitality I had thought about… so we can road-test that while we are in town as well."

"Oh, you are hilarious," she said with shake of her head. "Irene will be pleased to know that your spontaneous gestures of affection are as cold and calculated as an accountant."

"You, by the way, are sworn to secrecy. I require your full discrete cooperation… so that I am given all the credence of an impulsive admirer."

"I don't know of any such obligation. But okay, you have my full and complete 'discrete cooperation'. This is, by far, the most distracting and amusing thing that has happened since introducing Louisa Rilston to Pork Steaks. Your bounce has returned Mr Galloway. Perhaps this Irene is good for you."

"Perhaps she is."

Damn. There was that soft look again.

* * *

13.

When Sal emerged from her morning ablutions, Flynn had the kids making breakfast. The eggs were in various stages of frying. There was a flurry of energy that flagged something serious was afoot. "What's going on?"

"Breakfast," suggested Flynn evasively.

"Hmm. Really?"

"We're going shopping!" announced Philip excitedly.

"We are?"

"Yes!" confirmed Faith. "We are all getting new outfits... with new shoes!"

Salome's eyes flew wide open. She went to the stove and firmly pulled the pan off the heat and dragged Flynn outside to the verandah. "Why did you tell them that? I can't afford new clothes for them! Not now. My plan to get my house back is nearly complete. I can't just go spending willy-nilly!"

He leaned on the rail. The garden of poppies was growing. "We talked about this last night. This was your idea. I said we would get new outfits. We agreed on that."

"For Daisy!"

"You can't think I would buy Daisy new clothes and make them watch? That's cruel and absurd. I wouldn't do that without getting something for them as well."

"You don't have to buy my kids clothes. That's a lot."

"You are right. I don't have to. But you made the point about giving the impression that I am someone who cares. So… perhaps… that includes you and your family."

"Flynn you are not responsible for me… or my kids."

"I know that. But besides, it is nearly Christmas," he offered quickly.

She shook her head. "No. I can't afford to build their expectations that it might be like this every year."

"No, you are right. Can't have them wearing their Christmas presents around before the festive day, because then they will have nothing to open from under the tree. So, what if we call it a gift. A gift of appreciation. Is that allowed? Between friends?"

Sal closed her eyes and held her breath. "Friends?" Slowly, she let out her breath and sighed, shaking her head. "I don't know…"

"Or… perhaps it is better we call it a belated birthday present. The whole pox infestation ruined those festivities. We should celebrate that we all escaped with our lives to see another birthday. That is better. Make-up birthday presents."

"Flynn? What's going on?"

He shrugged and smiled. "I think you are right. My bounce is back."

"Oh, my goodness! Is this what being in-love looks like? Reckless and rash? Incoherent and irresponsible?"

"It has been a while, so I can barely remember…"

Oh dear. Well, it seems I will need to supervise you closely. I don't want you doing anything stupid that you will regret… in the interests of courting Lady Irene of course."

"Of course. I am counting on your good sense and tasteful guidance. Oh. And I need to buy a birthday gift for Irene as well... so I was hoping for your advice on that."

"I am going to have to charge you extra for consultancy fees."

"If you must. Toast is getting cold, and we have a big day ahead." He opened the door, and they went back inside. The kids were sitting at the table, staring with wide eyes. What they saw, must have so reassured them because they both erupted in a cheer, and Daisy started to cry from the shock of their loud applause.

* * *

Flynn quickly ordered a new shirt and pants, and then the seamstress sat little Daisy on her table and deftly checked some measurements. Miss Townsend chose a display book from her shelf and turned the page to some sketches of plain little frocks. Then she placed a few scraps of material over the drawing, inviting them to imagine what they may look like. She had fabric left over from other orders, and suggested that with these selections, she could run up three little frocks at a lower price.

Flynn looked at the samples and raised his brow. "I like the little daisy print, for obvious reasons. Maybe the blue... and I don't know... the green?"

"Green? Do you really want to dress your daughter in the colour of bile?" she whispered to Flynn behind her hand as Miss Townsend turned to put the book away. "Try this yellow – that is bright and happy," said Sal turning back to the scraps on the table.

"Yellow it is." There was only a little yellow left, but Miss Townsend was given full authority to add panels from the other bits and pieces. When that was sorted Flynn turned to Faith. "What do you like Faith?" he asked her.

The tape measure came out again. Faith chose a patterned fabric with a cherry print. Miss Townsend smiled with approval. "You have a decerning eye young lady. What buttons and ribbon trim would you like?"

"Oh, I don't think we need ribbon," interjected Sal.

"Nonsense. Ribbon is a must," assured Flynn. "It is for her birthday."

"Ma'ma? Can I?"

She took a deep breath. His insistence on using her kids to impress this Lady Irene was disturbing. It was obvious he was greatly invested in this coming visit. "Very well. If Miss Townsend thinks it will be an improvement."

"Oh, I do."

Faith looked a little overwhelmed at the array of colours. She went for a drab sort of grey with the very lowest price tag.

Flynn scoffed. "Nonsense! How can you pick a pretty fabric and then spoil the effect with that? Now Miss Townsend, flip over the tags, and let her just see the colours, from this side of the rack. That way, the price range is acceptable, and Faith, you can choose anything you like from that selection that will suit your dress."

Faith's shoulders visibly relaxed and she went for ribbon that matched the dark cherry-colour featured in the print. Then she chose buttons from the haberdashery rack that were the same colour.

Flynn looked exhilarated. "Excellent choice. Now Philip, what sort of fancy gear will you be wearing to church this Sunday?" Philip in all his boldness, now became shy, and went for plain dark brown pants and matching vest, finished with a white shirt... just like Flynn's. "Very grown up," he said with a slap on his shoulder. Philip beamed.

"Don't be encouraging tastes I will not be able to support Flynn."

"I wouldn't dare. Now what are you going to choose?"

"Me? I'm not ordering a new dress."

He raised his brow and smirked. "Are you sure? Haven't you also had a birthday? Besides, I would not have you jeopardise my good reputation. We have a code."

"You are taking my offer of support too far." Salome stared at him severely, and he matched her with a level gaze.

"My intention is to show my appreciation," he said quietly.

She took a breath. "Oh, very well." She looked through the old-fashioned pattern book offered by Miss Townsend... and then shook her head. "None of these are really suitable. I need simple. I also need a buttoned bodice... no frills." She took one basic style and stripped it of all embellishments.

Flynn was amused. "Oh, I do love a pragmatic choice. Not even one fashionable tuck or pleat?"

"It will not hinder your reputation if I choose a tidy modest style."

"True. I am sure that whatever you wear will be perfectly elegant,"

She shook her head and pointed to a darker blue fabric with a pattern through the weave. Miss Townsend assured her it was an excellent choice, hard wearing that washed easily. "Does this meet your satisfaction Mr Galloway?"

"Miss Townsend here is the authority on fabrics. As she has given it the nod, I will defer to her good taste. All she needs now is to write up the invoice. My job is done."

"Your job is only just starting. Don't forget we are still to order the highchair."

"Of course. And don't you forget we have shoes on our list as well," said Flynn with a smirk as Sal bundled the children out the door, and he bowed and counted out the cash onto Miss Townsend's dressmaking table.

The extravagance of this outing was overwhelming. They tackled the job of shoes with the bootmaker, and then they went over to Henrik's Workshop to order the highchair. The carpenter was a starched-and-dried German who spoke with a thick accent and had a perpetual frown on his brow. When they ordered the highchair, she insisted on practical. No fancy wood-turned features. Henrik covered the specifications of the highchair and quickly moved on to discuss Flynn's negotiations to buy into a partnership at the sawmill. Henrik declared the news of Flynn's involvement at the mill, gave him hope that his own timber orders would be streamlined. This energetic discussion took a while, and then it was time to collect their order from the grocer. It was a relief when they were ready to scramble into the buggy for home.

"Oh, I almost forgot. I need to buy a gift for Irene. This is very important. She has her birthday while she is with us over the weekend."

"Oh. Irene." Everything had been so amiable, that Sal almost forgot that this outing was entirely in support of the regrettable Irene's visit. "The children have just about had it, but very well... tell me what you had in mind."

"Well, I will bribe them with a treat, while we browse the displays in Bollinger's Jewellery Shop. There should be a suitable gift in there for sure."

She raised her brow. She could not remember the last time she set foot in this jewellery store. It was probably to purchase her wedding band. They settled the older two children on the back of the buggy with a toffee apple. It was pulled up by the curb, outside the jeweller's window, while they went inside.

"So, what were you thinking," she asked as they walked together along the glass cabinets. Sal adjusted Daisy on her hip looking at the displays with one eye on the children through the window.

"Something not too familiar, but still a gesture of regard."

"So...` not a necklace, or a bracelet, or a ring."

"Goodness no. This is the first time Irene is visiting the farm."

"So perhaps something useful might be suitable."

"Like...?"

"What did you buy Joy when you first showed interest in her?"

He grinned. "An ice-cream."

"Well... ice-cream is not on sale here. What about a brooch, or this pen? The embossed cap is really elegant."

"Oh yes, that is perfect. What style will I pick? What is your favourite colour?"

"Mine? I'm not sure how that is going to help Irene."

"Well, she is different to you in every way... so I would choose the opposite."

"I like practical."

"Yes of course... your dress is a practical blue. What about this?" He picked up another pen turning it over. The barrel of the pen had a collar made from the swirling dark green patterns of malachite stone.

"Not to my taste. The dark green style seems... manly. Something streamline, more feminine would be better."

"Hmm... green is definitely not your colour. What is to your taste then?"

"Most of these gifts are very ostentatious. I like this one... simple."

"The mother of pearl cap... yes, that is simply stunning. Wouldn't be to Irene's taste though, I am sure. I will go with this one. Do you agree that the floral enamel is ladylike? There. One practical gift. That was relatively painless." While Mr Bollinger gift wrapped the box, they continued to analyse the various items on display while they waited.

By the time they were driving home, the children's enthusiasm for their day in town had waned. Daisy was whingy; Philip was fractious; and Faith cried and hit back when Philip poked her. Sal sighed. Sometimes the end of a day didn't match the beginning.

* * *

14.

But Flynn didn't head out of town. Instead, he turned up the street towards Mrs Trimboli's.

Salome frowned. "Do you think visiting is the best idea at the moment?"

"The very best. I asked Mrs Trimboli to cook us an early dinner. The kids are tired and hungry. This is quicker... and very much in the interests of a calmer evening. And it gives me a chance to do a tenancy check-in at your place. You settle the kids... feed Daisy... and I will attend to the check-in." With that, he disappeared.

When Sal walked in, Mrs Trimboli had the table set, and a big pot of spaghetti on the stove. Mrs Trimboli had a way of making her always feel welcome. While Sal helped the kids wash their hands, the plates were served, and they said grace. A calm settled over the table as they slurped their pasta, and Sal could feel herself relax. They sat and chatted about all the things they had done on their shopping day... including the wonderful toffee apple treat.

Eventually Mrs Trimboli stood up and cleared the plates. "It's getting late mia cara. Why don't you throw the little ones through the bath? They've had a big day."

"I have no idea where Flynn is. He said he was going to check in with the tenants. But he's been gone a long time. I hope there is no problem. Perhaps I should run over and check everything is okay."

"Oh, I wouldn't bother. If there is a problem, you will know soon enough. I will read to the older two when they finish their bath... and you can have a bath with Daisy. Then you will be refreshed as well. Clean towels are in the spare room."

Salome didn't even feel like arguing. It saved the trouble of doing it when they got home. She got in the old clawfoot bath and played with Daisy for a bit. Mrs Trimboli came in with a towel and wrapped Daisy in it. "The children are looking through a book; you relax for a spell while I dress the little one. You've had a big day..."

Salome stretched out, soaking away her fatigue, and sighed. The woman was a saint. She said a grateful prayer. Perhaps God had answered her plea. This year had started out to sink her, but in so many ways it had turned out fuller and more satisfying than she could have ever imagined. How was that possible when the whole world was struggling in so many ways? The only fly in the ointment was this pending visit from Lady Irene. How she wished she had the courage to...

Mrs Trimboli knocked at the door. "Flynn is here. He is having dinner now."

"Oh okay. I won't be long." When she came out, Flynn was sitting at the table. She frowned. "I thought you went over to check how the Flannigan's were going with the house."

"They are fine. No issues."

"Why are you all dressed up?"

"Went home to attend to the chores. Thought I might as well change. After all, you promised to road-test an activity of country hospitality for me."

"I did? Oh yes. I had forgotten that. Really? You still want to do that?"

"I most certainly do."

She sat down suspiciously. "What does this road-test involve? A drive?"

"A dance. You are going to take me dancing."

"That's ridiculous. I don't dance. Well, not for a long time, at least."

"Remember you swore allegiance to help me. A dance may not be a suitable activity, but until we try, how will I know if I can hold my own on the dance floor?"

"Well, it would have been helpful if you had told me this before we left home. You are dressed up; I can't go in this. I have nothing to wear."

"You have a new dress. We bought it today remember."

"Miss Townsend said it would take at least a week before our orders will be ready."

"I paid to put a push on that part of the order. It cost extra, but it is ready for you."

She sighed. "Oh Flynn... what are you doing? You cannot possibly be this nervous about Irene. You tick every box of an eligible husband, and you are very capable at whatever you set your mind to. You don't have to take me dancing to prove this."

"I think I do. Please. The dress cost extra. And the children are settled."

Mrs Trimboli came and took her hand, pulling her to her feet. "Come. Get changed. Allow this young man a dance to reassure himself if that is what he needs. You might have fun as well."

Salome paused. It sounded appealing... like the warm bath she had just spent soaking away all the irritable moments at the end of a day. She smiled at the impossibility of having a night out. "Sure. Why not..."

"Your dress is hanging in the 'robe... in the spare room."

"Mrs Trimboli, did you know about this all along?"

"It amuses an old lady, to see someone have a surprise. Go... it is a beautiful dress."

Salome took a moment and then nodded. She put on the dress, and stockings. Her shoes had been polished while she was in the bath. Mrs Trimboli brought in a small leather case with a wink. "I borrowed this from my daughter-in-law. A little bit of lip colour, and perfume, and you will be the princess of the ball."

"Mrs Trimboli, you do understand that Flynn is testing out an idea for his visitor. This is not a date."

"Pfft. Who will know?"

"I know."

"Sure... and then you come home when it is over. So just pretend. There is no harm in it."

When she came out of the room, there was a was a pause... and Flynn nodded and murmured his appreciation. He even required her to do a twirl, modelling her new dress. Then he produced a box. "I understand flowers are an important aspect to these occasions. I had a sample made. Do you think it is suitable?" He opened the box and laid a corsage on the table.

"Oh... for Irene?"

"Well, do you think it would appeal?"

"You have good taste Mr Galloway. The simple white flowers with blue ribbon suit my outfit perfectly. Be reassured of your ability to choose flowers." She looked at it curiously.

He shrugged unperturbed. "I am found out. They tell me white poppies are the flowers of peace. Since Ivy is your middle name, I couldn't resist adding a touch of ivy. Also means peace..." He pinned the simple arrangement on Salome's lapel and stood back in admiration. "Just beautiful. Peace suits you."

He bowed gallantly to Mrs Trimboli with a flourish. "I thank you for your gracious conspiring for this evening's outing." He turned to Salome and held out his elbow. "Shall we?"

She laughed with a shake of her head. "You are going to a lot of effort Mr Galloway. Miss Irene has no idea how you have targeted her in your sights. You have me convinced that she will be lucky to escape."

"It is not my plan to go to all this trouble, just to have my intentions come to naught. Come, let's get out of here before we wake the children up."

As they pulled up outside the hall, a wave of uncertainty hit Salome like a wall. She sat frozen as Flynn came around to help her down from the buggy and offered her his hand. She shook her head and stared straight ahead. "Flynn. I'm not sure this is a good idea. You know what people think."

"I know what I think. We have done nothing wrong."

"But technically they don't know that."

"Would you suggest I announce to the entire assembly that I live a celibate life and your virtue is unsullied?"

She laughed, partly out of shock and nerves. "You are not being helpful. I am trying to protect you."

"I would suggest that the best protection you can offer is to help my plan be as rehearsed as possible. I want it to go smoothly."

"But to turn up with me... and then Irene. It is providing more fuel for the gossip that your life is morally loose. Think how this will impact Daisy."

"Sal... do you really believe that I would jeopardise Daisy's wellbeing in anyway?"

"No, of course not. I know that. But I also fear that your reputation has taken some hits. And that is something you were very definite about, right from the beginning."

"Are you refusing to come inside with me? Do we dance out here with the horse and buggies?"

"Okay... I will go, but this is more difficult than I ever imagined."

"Well... since our purpose is to submit very aspect of this outing to a road test... all is not lost. Apparently, getting inside is an unexpected ordeal, so what if we agree to just one dance and then leave? That would give us more data to work with, than sitting here at the gate."

"Well, okay. One dance."

"Or perhaps two. It has been a long time. Irene apparently has a particular fondness for dances."

"Ahh. I see." She nodded and braced herself, clinging to Flynn's arm like a lifebuoy that was preventing her from sinking.

They walked inside and the music was playing energetically. Already the dance floor was full of partners swinging around in time to the beat. There were a few nods, and a few turned heads, and a few voices that dropped to a whisper as they walked around the parameter of the hall.

The dance finished and the couples clapped, and the next dance was announced. Flynn held out his hand. "Let's just bite the bullet. A little bit of jazz should be a fair test, even if this is the only dance we manage tonight." He took her hand and led her to the floor. He looked down at her and smiled. "Am I doing okay?"

She nodded. "Yes, I believe so. Perhaps dancing is like riding a horse, and you just need to get back in the saddle."

He took a few tentative steps. "Well... let's see how we go. I don't feel as confident as you apparently do. It has been a long while since this tormented widower has danced." Salome easily followed his lead. He raised his brow and stepped out again. She followed his steps again. He tightened his hold and stepped out in time with the music. Soon they were dancing across the floor in synchronised synergy as the music enveloped them. Salome felt the vitality of the moment. She felt the rhythm. She felt the haunting jazz melody drawing her forward. She felt her body warm from his touch, as they were moving together. She watched his face softened into a grin. "Oh my! Irene is going to love this..." he murmured as he smiled at her again. And the music in Salome's head came to a squealing, screeching halt. She blinked hard, mis-stepped, and stood awkwardly on Flynn's shoe. He caught her under her back as she gasped and stumbled.

She blushed brightly, as she stood up, pulled away and retreated from the floor, embarrassed. Flynn looked at her cautiously as he followed her. "Hey... sorry. Did I step on you? I thought we were doing okay."

"We were. You. You were doing great. I misjudged my step, and that threw me. I wasn't paying attention." Oh boy. She really was not paying attention. Not at all. How could she forget herself so thoroughly!

"Oh. Okay."

"Look, would you mind if we went home? It is very late. The kids are going to be a mess tomorrow."

"Mrs Trimboli was going to make swags up for them... and the spare bed for you. I'll come by and pick you all up in the morning. There is time for another dance. My foot has fully recovered."

"I..." Salome stopped and blinked. "No... I don't think so. I'd better get back, so Mrs Trimboli is not waiting up for me. But thank you."

"Well, if you are sure..."

"I am. And Flynn? The dance was lovely. You are a very good dancer. You have no need to worry. Irene is in safe hands."

* * *

15.

For the entire time Flynn was away at work, Salome struggled to prepare for this up-coming visit. She vacillated between nervous anxiety and frustrated anger. She so desperately didn't want to care. Yet, undeniably, she did. She didn't want Irene coming and stealing his heart away forever. Flynn had called her a friend. A friend. She had never even considered that being his friend would ever be an option, so to come to the realisation that this friendship was one that she desperately wanted to protect, was a shock. Something unexpected had locked in as they danced. And now, on top of that, she suspected that being his friend was hardly enough.

One conversation played over and over in her mind in the quiet moments when the kids were still. The silence of his house echoed with those words, *"You and me... that is never going to happen."* That stirred up a blustery tempest of emotion, and she wished she could unhear the determination in his voice. *"You are not in the running."* She hadn't wanted it. She had avoided it. Yet the man had insisted on being kind, and helpful, and supportive, and considerate, and... damn it... a very good dancer!

That taunted her. How could someone who casually considered her a friend, be kinder and more respectful than the man who vowed to love and protect her as a husband? That still didn't make sense. But she was certain that she preferred Flynn's friendship, however benign, over anything Pedro ever offered as a husband.

There was another thing she was certain of. There was no way, anyone in their right mind would ever let him get away. Irene certainly

106

wouldn't. She felt it in her bones. Salome's days at Bottlebrush Grove were numbered... and she grieved the loss of something that had been profoundly enriching. She grieved losing Daisy and her bright little smile that lit up when she snuggled her in the morning. She grieved missing all the wonderful things that Philip would rush into the house bursting to tell her from his explorations around the farm. She grieved the quiet elegance that seemed to settle over Faith like a shawl, decades older than her short nine years. She even grieved feeding greedy Pork Steaks. And then she stopped herself, dazed. She never mourned her husband – full stop. She had felt sad that the idea of them as a couple was never great, but in the end, it was more of a relief. Even that never compared to the intensity of what she was feeling now. She was sure that had to be inappropriate and weird. Flynn employed her to look after his daughter and his animals. Nothing more.

Salome wondered if she had the courage to follow her children's lead and sabotage Irene's stay. It had been effective for Louisa's visit. But Flynn's manner had been so different around this visit, that he would end up despising her if he ever caught wind her of agenda. Part of her wanted to poison Irene's food... another part wanted to stand up like the battle champions of ancient Greece who stood before the ageless walls of Troy and fight honourably against the onslaught that threatened their home. She shook her head. No. That was way too dramatic. She was usually so sensible. If she really did regard Flynn well... then she had to step back and allow him to make his choice. And she already knew his choice was Irene. Irene who loved to dance.

So, in the end, she readied for this visit. She washed the bed linen and was grateful Philip hadn't wet the bed this week. She made up Faith's bed and aired the room and tidied the house. She prepared Flynn's favourite menu and tried not to think too much about Irene being there also.

She drove the children in to visit Mrs Trimboli on the Friday. She sat down at her table with a sigh, while the children went to tell the chickens how much they were missed.

Salome shook her head. "What am I going to do Mrs Trimboli? Flynn has been acting so weird. This time he is actually in love. I know it. And I... I feel sad that my time at Bottlebrush Grove is over. I just want it to go on and on..." It was a relief to confess it out loud. There. She said it. She didn't want to go.

Mrs Trimboli sat down and took her hand. "I know mia cara. I know. I feel like a collaborator of the worst kind... agreeing to mind the children so this Irene can visit. But I have given my word... and I pray The Good Shepherd will guide his sheep and keep them safe. You're one of his little lambs, my beautiful Salom-ee."

Sal smiled sadly and noticed a dull ache in her chest. A tear trembled on her lashes. "I have no idea how I am going to do this. I have to be a civil hostess, and all I want to do is scratch out her eyes."

"Just be your wonderful, gracious self, and perhaps she will be like the other one... the city one who came before, and she will not like it here, and go home."

"Well, it probably would not matter anyway. If it wasn't Louisa, and if it is not Irene... it will be someone else for sure. The man has made it very clear he is out on the market for a wife. It will only be a matter of time."

Mrs Trimboli stood up to check the lasagne in her oven, made from the vegetables in her garden, and a smattering of rabbit mince. It smelt amazing. Sal went to change Daisy's nappy. Then she called the children in to have morning tea. When Sal finished her cup of tea, she said goodbye to the children, collected the highchair from the carpenter, and went back home to finish her preparations for dinner. Sal changed into her new dress and checked the dinner roasting in the oven once more. She adjusted the flowers that Faith had picked and repositioned the vase. She fed Daisy... and put on her new quaint little daisy outfit. She paced around, rocking Daisy over her shoulder as if she was a newborn with a bad case of cholic.

Flynn found her still pacing when he opened the door. He had a suitcase in both hands and a broad smile on his face. "Good evening! We have arrived," he announced.

Oh boy. It had started.

"The train was a little late, but all in all, it seems Irene's travel was not too uncomfortable. Salome, let me introduce you to my... Irene. Irene, this is Salome. And this is Daisy."

Really? *My* Irene? Sal bobbed her head in acknowledgement. "Welcome to Bottlebrush Grove Irene." Was it awful to say a bold-faced lie if you offer it in a polite tone? She wasn't welcome at all.

Irene had light brown hair. Mid height. Unremarkable features, but a pleasant face. Her dress was modest; tasteful; modern. All of the pretentiousness she had noticed in Louisa was missing. Huh. That was a shame.

"Well, I guessed you would be tired from travelling, so I have dinner ready to go."

"Wonderful. It smells amazing. I brought a bottle of wine," said Flynn which he produced with a flourish.

Irene shook her head and smiled at his theatrics. "Well, I will wash up. Thank you, Salome. You are right... I am very tired, so just a very small serve for me."

"Oh. Okay. I anticipated you would be hungry."

"No not really. I ate at one of the comfort-stops."

"Oh." Sal raised her brow. Perhaps she was a fragile sort. "Well, um... I will start, I guess. Flynn – can you hold Daisy?"

"Sure! Just so you know... I am famished. So don't be stingy in my serves. I have been looking forward to this all week." He showed Irene to Faith's room, chatting comfortably about... trivia.

"Hmm." Sal glowered as she watched him go. There was that bounce again. She took a deep breath, then brought down the best crockery from the hutch and started to serve out. Irene joined Flynn where he was playing with Daisy, her little face alight with giggles. Wouldn't it be something if Daisy had been screaming and fractious this evening? But no, just according to her luck, she was delightful and enchanting, full of smiles. While Sal served out the potatoes and roast pumpkin, she watched Irene play with Daisy, using a rattle to keep time with a nursery rhyme she was singing.

Then Irene disappeared and came back holding a little present. "I know her first birthday is coming up, and I wanted to give her something." Sal watched as Daisy ripped at the paper and extracted a cute bear with button eyes. Daisy laughed, and chewed the paper and smiled, and cooed, and ahhed. Already they were the perfect family. Sal blinked back tears.

When she looked up, Flynn was looking at her curiously. He handed Daisy to Irene and came over. "Can I help you with anything?"

"No, I am just about done." Done. Really done.

"Well okay. Here, let me carry the plates." He paused for a moment, then picked them up with a slight shake of his head and took them to the table. He gathered some stemmed glasses from the china cabinet and uncorked the wine. Sal took Daisy and settled her in the highchair. Flynn said grace and poured the wine. They had barely started when Irene placed her serviette on the table. "I am so sorry, but I really am exhausted. Could I be excused to retire?"

"Oh. Yes. Okay. Do you need anything?" Sal asked with concern.

"No. Not at all. I really do appreciate your hospitality, Salome. It is lovely to be here."

Flynn didn't look at all disturbed by her rudeness. He just stood, kissed her on the cheek, and wished her good night as she left. He settled in to finish his meal, and to sip his wine.

Sal leant over. "Don't you think that is odd?" she whispered.

"No, the meal is perfect. You have done well."

"I mean Irene. Who leaves company after such a short time when they are visiting? I made pudding."

"Well, she did say she was tired."

"Yes – but she is visiting to be here with *you*. I just think it is... unusual." Rude actually. Irene got a poor grade on that one.

"She doesn't leave until Sunday afternoon. Plenty of time to catch up." And he leant over and topped up her wine glass. "Just let her sleep. I cannot let this excellent food go to waste. This is great. Have I ever told you, that you are quite the cook Salome."

"Thank Mrs Trimboli for that. I can't master her Italian dishes, but she gave me many pointers on usual things that I found impossible when I was first married. Mind you, cooking in your oven is so much easier than mine. The one at home is old; it smokes like a curing oven and burns unevenly. I've had to become adept at rotating everything."

Flynn passed another piece of roasted pumpkin to Daisy. He adjusted her bib and laughed as she began to smash it on the highchair tray. "The chair is now officially broken in. I think Henrik did a good job. Are you happy with it?"

"I only picked it up today. But it is certainly easier than a pile of books. I have restocked your bookshelf, so your little library is back in order."

"And I do like the daisy print dress. Good choice. She looks like a picture. Very pretty, little Daisy!" He asked about the animals... and they easily fell into their normal way of talking. The wine tasted good, and the meal continued in a pleasant tone. Eventually she stirred. "Did you want dessert? I can save it for tomorrow if you prefer..."

"Sure, save a portion. But I am up for some now. What did you make?"

"Bread and butter pudding..."

"Are you tormenting me with all my favourites? I can't leave that to go to Pork Steaks. It is always best straight from the oven."

"Then, dessert coming up..."

"This is absolutely delicious," he said, tasting the pudding. They lingered over their wine. Flynn paused and put down his glass. "Salome... I trust you know that I very much appreciate what you do for Daisy and myself."

"Well... you do pay me."

"Yes, but I am also very aware, that what you do is over and above what is agreed. Everything is done so excellently. Like dinner tonight. You have gone to much effort to make everything perfect. And it really is. Thank you."

She smiled and shook her head with a giggle. The wine had lightened her head and her mood. What had been a slight against Flynn's hospitality was now just funny. "Except for one tiny detail. Irene abandoned ship and left you to eat alone. Your navigated course as captain of this ship did not dock at its desired destination."

"Well not completely alone. You are here...my co-pilot... and Daisy... my little first-mate."

"Co-pilot? Not deck-hand and mess-cook?"

"Even though Irene decided to forgo such an excellent meal, fine dining and amiable conversation is never wasted. I have enjoyed tonight. Very much."

"There's a pattern developing here Mr Galloway. Your lady guests seem to be consistently of the mind to desert you, in spite of your best laid plans. Let's hope that tomorrow you will be allowed to offer at least some of your strategic hospitality."

"I'm sure it will be fine. Oh... by the way. I invited my overseer to join us for our picnic tomorrow... down by the creek. I thought that would make a pleasant group."

"You invited your overseer... the hardworking, good looking one? What are you up to Flynn? I said no matchmaking."

"Hmm. You did. But he misses his family... working away a lot."

"He's married? Oh grief. You also said 'single'!"

"No... no. I mean his sister and mother have gone visiting. No wife; it's just them. He wanted to get away for a bit."

"To his boss's place? Are you sure this is helping him?"

"Options are limited, when you are overworked and under-paid. But he likes kids... and he was keen to see the farm. I was thinking of selling him a horse. We can pick him up when we go in and collect the children from Mrs Trimboli tomorrow."

"But I arranged for them to stay for a couple of days. To give you space. Wasn't that the idea?"

"Sure. We had space tonight. Lovely. But there is no way we can have a picnic by the creek without them. Philip would never forgive me."

She laughed. "You're right: he might not. But this seems to be turning out quite different to your idea of a quiet romantic weekend for two."

"It can be romantic if you want it to be. His name is Simon James." He laughed at the look of disgust on her face.

Sal shook her head. "I can assure you right now... nothing will happen, no matter how handsome you think Mr Simon James might be... or how accommodating of children you suppose he is."

"Sounds like the perfect catch. Don't you like handsome and hardworking?"

"I like you."

"Do you now? Well, I might rub off on him, and his appeal might increase."

"It won't. Be reassured of that."

"Okay... but still we need some things for our picnic tomorrow. Fresh bread – with plenty of ragged edges. Apricot jam, mulberry pie and some biscuits. Billy tea."

"Why don't we take some potatoes and bake them in the campfire coals?"

"That's the most fantastic idea! Mud Spuds. I haven't had them for a very long time! You are on!"

"Oh. Are you sure? Mud? Do you think Irene would mind something like that?"

"Well, I don't know... but there is one way to find out. So, if we are cooking potatoes, we'll do some cobs of corn in the billy as well. Butter and ground pepper. Great picnic idea."

"You are a bold suitor Mr Galloway. I will give you that. You hold nothing back."

* * *

16.

Surprisingly, the children were packed up ready to go when they arrived in the morning to collect them. Sal had anticipated whinges and dragging feet, because they were being taken from their stayover at Mrs Trimboli's before their allotted time. But she had none of that. Sal placed the large jars of fresh milk on the bench she had brought with her. A young man in a brown vest sat at Mrs Trimboli's table with a full breakfast plate before him.

"Mr James... would you like some coffee? One of my sons brought me some freshly roasted beans."

"Oh yes please! It smells wonderful."

She pulled her largest mug from the shelf and filled it to the brim. "Milk, fresh this morning?"

"Yes Ma'am. Thank you."

"Flynn? Coffee? Yes? Salome?"

"I... umm... sure." She sat at the bench away from the table.

Flynn asked Simon some work-related questions and soon the men were deep into some issue with a current work order. Salome watched them intrigued. This was Flynn at work. She'd seen some glimpses of it before... like at the bank or Henrik's workshop. Usually, he was just Flynn. Daisy's father. The Landlord. The animal lover. Her friend. She swallowed a mouth full of coffee.

Mrs Trimboli pulled up a stool to sit beside her. "So where is the lady? Has she already left?" she asked quietly.

"No. Irene wanted to take this morning easy and do some reading. Flynn seemed okay to leave her there by herself. She is not what I would call high maintenance. She is very even-tempered." She sighed. Another point of disappointment. She really wanted to dislike her, but as Irene helped with the breakfast and pitched in with the dishes, Sal was struggling not to appreciate her pleasant nature.

"Oh... so...? How did your dinner go?"

Sal shrugged bewildered. "She barely ate anything, and then she went to bed just as we started."

"So, the dinner was wasted..." Mrs Trimboli shook her head and tut-tutted.

"Well, Flynn and I had a lovely time. He even brought wine."

"Oh... wine? With the handsome Mr Galloway... alone? Without children... or a guest."

Sal shook her head. "No, it wasn't like that. I just wish it was..."

Mrs Trimboli looked thoughtfully at the two sitting at her table deep in conversation. "Mr James seems a nice young man."

"Yes, he does..."

"I wonder if Miss Irene... would be partial to those handsome blue eyes of his?"

"Mrs Trimboli... what are you suggesting?"

"I'm just saying... if they did get talking... or walking... it would be convenient if Flynn was not around to distract them. You could distract *him*..."

"Oh..." She took another sip of coffee and considered them both sitting at the table. Suddenly Simon James was not the enemy. Perhaps Simon was what this picnic by the creek really needed after all.

As soon as coffee was finished, they piled into the buggy and Simon followed them on his saddle horse. They arrived, greeted by the boisterous welcome of Rusty. Irene was sitting on the verandah, relaxed and immersed in her book. It took Sal a moment to gather herself. The picture of Irene sitting there, elegantly presiding over her house, was so wrong. But she forced a smile and checked herself. Flynn's house. Daisy's house. Not her house. She took a breath, paused, and determined she would go with Mrs Trimboli's plan of distraction.

Irene came down the verandah stairs and introduced herself to the children as they climbed down from the buggy. By then Simon had ridden up and dismounted. Flynn made the introductions. It seemed to Sal that Simon James lingered just a little too long over Miss Irene's hand. Flynn hadn't noticed as he had already taken the kids' bags in his hands and was herding them into the house.

Sal followed him closely behind. She pulled him aside. "Flynn! Where are the children going to sleep? Irene is in Faith's bed."

"Irene can sleep my room, so Faith can have her bed back."

"Oh. Your room..."

"Yes. I will take the swag. In the living room." He grinned. "Still celibate. For now."

"It is a shame that the rest of the world does not give you credit for being the honourable man that you are Flynn Galloway."

"They don't need to. As long as the people who count do." He paused and looked at her. He went to say something else, when Philip came careering inside, jumped over Daisy crawling on the floor and bumped into them in a single move.

"Philip! Walk inside. What if you tripped over Daisy? You wouldn't want to run her down," she cautioned.

"Sure…" and he went to run off.

Flynn reached out and reined him in by the collar. "Philip. Listen to your mother. I am learning to do that. Take it easy."

"Yes Sir."

Flynn nodded, as Philip walked, very quickly, to the back door and then escaped. Salome looked at Flynn's back as he put the bags on the kids' beds. She felt strange, almost as if the wind had been knocked out of her. He came out of the room; he looked at her and smiled. She shook herself, took a breath, and went to prepare the things for the picnic.

"I've got a couple of things that I need an extra pair of hands for, so while I have Simon here, I'll get those jobs out of the way. We will be back around one, and then we can go down to the creek after lunch."

It sounded like he was asking her for… permission… or input… or something. It was his weekend. His date. She was just his employee. "Sure. I have things to get ready so that works well. I will be sorted by the time you get back."

Sal gathered the things she thought they might need and assembled the boxes on the verandah. Irene was happy to play with Daisy, and she consulted with Faith and Philip about all sorts of serious matters like ants' nests, and butterfly wings and fungi growing on wooden fence posts. They gave her all the intimate details of their bout of chicken pox, describing how Ma'ma had made an oatmeal paste to paint their spots. And they had used an artist brush to play join the dots and create all sorts of pictures in oatmeal body-paint. Faith had painted various animals in Philip's dots. His favourite was a portrait of Rusty the dog. Philip had covered Faith's body in a variety of patterns that were actually amazing scientific inventions. Irene came inside laughing. "Oh, it is wonderful here! I see why you love it so much. This is the perfect place to bring up a family."

Sal looked at her and determined again that she needed to keep the enemy close. She poured a cup of tea. "So where did you two meet?" Sal asked casually pushing it toward her.

"We have been corresponding for some time. It was Flynn's idea to meet up in person at the farm here. It has been the best idea."

"Oh. What sort of things do you write about... in your letters?"

"Oh... well... my job, I guess. I am a schoolteacher, so that is an endless source of amusing stories. I had one student say to me last week that I reminded her of... wait for it... her grandmother's slippers! Her grandmother's slippers? I could not think of anything less flattering," she laughed. "But when I asked her why I would remind her of them, she said most seriously that her grandmother only ever wears her slippers inside because she feels at home in them. She said that is how she feels at school every day... safe and comfy like at her grandmother's house. I know things are difficult at home for her, so suddenly that rather insulting metaphor was transformed into the greatest compliment. If children can feel comfortable learning, then that is going to encourage them, not just to do their homework, but to become lifelong learners."

"Oh wow... yes. I guess that is true." To add insult to injury, Irene was smart and insightful.

"I notice your Philip has the most inquiring mind. And little Faith – how bright and articulate she is for someone so young. You have done well with your children Salome."

Sal smiled. It didn't matter just now that she had resolved to dislike this person. She complimented her children. "Thank you, Irene. I appreciate you taking time to talk with them."

"Why wouldn't I? They are great."

"Oh well, you know... being here to meet up for a quiet weekend together... and finding us all here."

"Oh, don't worry about it. Flynn was very definite about what to expect. He said you were all going to be here. And the same with Simon."

"Oh. Well... nice to have no surprises, I guess."

"Oh, that is just it – it is a surprise. Flynn's told me about this place so often... but I never imagined it would be so wonderful. It's perfect. So, what can I do to help get ready for this afternoon?"

"Just having the children talking with you is a great help. That means they are not busy undoing what I am preparing. I might give them both something to eat now..." She called them in, gave them a sandwich and a drink. By the time they finished, Flynn and Simon appeared, and they had their lunch. Flynn harnessed his horse and cart, and they loaded it up with their boxes, and they made their way down to the creek.

The kids headed straight for the water and started to repair their dam and steppingstones. Philip was disappointed that his tadpoles and guppies had escaped the pond they had made and went on a hunt to repopulate it. Faith set about restoring her water garden with fresh duckweed. Irene took Daisy down to the creek for a splash and Simon followed her while Flynn helped Sal set up the picnic.

"You know, I used to bring Joy here. She really liked it. She would come here to paint. When you said this was the outing you thought would be appreciated... that is what I thought of."

"Oh... I hope you do not mind. I would hate to think that in some way we have contaminated those memories for you."

"Contaminated? No. I would say... building on them. I would love Daisy to become as familiar with this little spot as her mother was. You are right about that. This is part of her story... part of ours. I can't ignore that."

She looked over Flynn's shoulder and saw Simon talking with Irene. Oh. Distraction time. When Flynn turned to join them down by the creek, Sal took a breath and quickly cleared her throat. "Ah Flynn, I was wondering about firewood. We will have to start cooking the Mud Spuds soon if we want to eat before dark. Would you like me to help you?"

"Firewood?" He looked at her and slowly nodded. "Sure... I could do with some help." He pulled the axe from the cart and slung it over his shoulder.

Sal looked at him, all very relaxed and self-possessed, and burst out laughing. "I just remembered you're a lumberjack by trade. You must think me odd to suggest I help with the firewood. I'm sorry... that was very strange."

His eyes lit up at her laughter. "I never say no to an extra pair of arms to carry. Or... perhaps you were devising a plan to have some time alone with me... away from the others." She blushed and he winked with a grin. "I won't tell."

"Flynn Galloway... your charm won't work on me."

"Ah, but it already has. After all, you offered to carry firewood. That is no small transaction to one who does lumber for a living."

"Very well. I am at your service. Even though I have thoroughly embarrassed myself. Let's get to it, or our potatoes will never be cooked.

* * *

Flynn pushed up a bank of live coals to the side of the improvised fire-pit. The kids had been on a mission to find some smooth sticky mud for the potatoes. When they were satisfied that they had found the perfect mud on the opposite bank of the creek, they grabbed Simon, who took the shovel and helped them fill a bucket. Together they slathered each potato in an even thick wad of smooth clay-mud, and then, when that job was done, they proceeded to cover themselves all over. Irene stood watching in amazement, laughing at their antics when she was splattered with the overflow. Using bushman tongs of two green sticks, Flynn positioned each potato in the hot coals. They sizzled and hissed as he banked more coals around and over them.

The kids ran screaming with laughter down to the creek and rolled on the gravelly creek bed and watched the shallow water run muddy-red as they washed off. Salome produced a bar of soap, and scrubbed each muddy little body including their hair, towelled them dry and then dressed them in clean, dry clothes. They came up to the campfire as the sun was starting to set. They had a warm drink, and a warm blanket to share amazing stories to recap their afternoon adventures, while the billy boiled, and the corn cobs bobbed in the pot. Flynn produced a flat metal plate and positioned it over the fire; Sal threw on some fresh steaks; Irene retrieved the dinner plates from the cart.

Soon Flynn was extracting the Mud Spuds from the fire. The mud casing was baked hard, and using a flat rock, he tapped each one and cracked off the protective casing. The mud fell off in leaving each baked potato clean as a whistle. The corn cobs were extracted from the billy, their plates piled with barbequed steak, buttered baked spuds and corn on the cob. A feast! Philip was amazed; Faith was impressed; Irene was delighted; and Simon was obviously becoming more and more attached to the lovely Irene. He sat with her, attended to her, joked with her, talked with her. Salome was too busy to intervene any further with strategies of distraction, but it didn't seem necessary as Flynn sat helping the kids navigate their meal while sitting on a log. They were guessing who was going to get smoke in their eyes when the breeze changed next, wondering if it really did mean that they were the prettiest person around the campfire. Salome watched them from the corner of her eye as she mashed up one of the soft centres of the bush baked potatoes to feed Daisy, and she pushed her wistful thoughts away. Tonight, she would take Mrs Trimboli's advice: *Just pretend. There is no harm in it. You come home when it is all over.* What harm was there if she pretended that Flynn was here for her, and lady Irene was as smitten with Mr James as he obviously was with her?

After they had eaten, they all laid back and stared at the stars. Every so often someone would gasp and point to a falling star. Flynn leant over and directed Faith's arm to some fireflies blinking their gentle white light in and out of the trees. "Oh!" she gasped. "The stars really have fallen! They are so pretty!" Philip jumped up with a mission to catch some and they bounced and chased the elusive fireflies together.

Eventually they came back to the fire. Philip was discouraged that this firefly mission was unsuccessful, because all he managed to catch was a couple of tiny black bugs. Irene gently explained that their light went out when they were squashed. Philip vowed never to catch a firefly ever again, but to stand tall as a valiant protector of all future generations of fireflies forever. And with that resolution, it was like the day caught up with them and the children both snuggled in their blankets by the fire to tell fantastic stories. But the very act of being still, gave their exhausted little bodies permission to sleep, and the next sentence of their wonderful tales were never spoken.

They sat around the fire for a long while, just telling stories, and watching the stars, and the logs in the fire collapse on themselves, shedding a shower of sparks that swirled up into the night. Eventually Salome reluctantly stirred. She handed a sleeping Daisy over to Irene to hold while she packed up the picnic boxes. The dying fire was doused in water. Flynn bundled the sleeping children into the back of the cart. Simon walked ahead of the horse with a lantern held high, and they tracked their way back home.

* * *

17.

"Flynn tells me it is your birthday today," said Sal when Irene emerged from Flynn's room glowing as fresh as if she had walked straight out of the framed pages of a lady's magazine.

She blushed prettily. "Oh yes. This has already been the most perfect birthday. I enjoyed last night so much. Although, I felt a little guilty that Simon had to ride back into town to stay at Mrs Trimboli's place."

"Oh, it is not far really. I'm sure he was fine. And Mrs Trimboli is a wonderful hostess. Simon assured me he will be back again for lunch. So, this morning the children and I have a mission to bake you a birthday cake. I was planning a butter cake that has a Mrs Trimboli twist. My old oven always dried out any cakes I attempted, so she showed me a perfect trick to retrieve the most terrifying failures. The kids loved it so much that I pretty much can't bake any cake without doing this now. The question is – what fruit do you like? I have some mulberry or apricot preserves that I wrangled from Mrs Trimboli's pantry... or some lemon butter."

"Oh, this is so intriguing. I have to say lemon sounds delicious."

"Lemon cake it is. That is our birthday gift to you... and you are welcome to join us if you would like. Cooking with children is always an adventure. I've started the bread... and the dough is on its first rising. The kids are out with Flynn milking the cow... so breakfast won't be long."

Daisy starting to stir, and Sal nodded for Irene to pick her up. She sat Daisy in the highchair and Irene started to feed her strained porridge with mashed apricot preserve. Irene laughed. "Oh, she likes this! She really does. Yes, yes... I'm coming with another spoonful..."

"It is one of her favourites. I can show you how to make it. Daisy will always eat that even if she refuses everything else." Sal turned away and rushed out to the laundry to attend to the muddy clothes and towels from yesterday's antics. She gagged and gasped as a wave of sadness hit her. Irene was perfect. She was lovely and kind. She could not choose a better mother for Daisy... or wife for Flynn. It didn't matter if the handsome Simon James was smitten. She felt a little guilty that she had encouraged that triangle as Simon was about to have his heart broken. She had no doubt that Flynn would win out. Of course he would. She flushed her face with cool water and filled up the tub to rinse off the clothes stained with mud, and left them there to soak, along with a bucket full of nappies. She squared her shoulders, took a breath, and braced herself for cake baking escapades.

After the breakfast dishes were washed, Flynn made himself scarce as he had some fencing repairs to attend to. Salome lined the kids up along the table and each was given a job to do. Faith had the butter and sugar to mix. Philip was given the flour to sift. Philip cracked the eggs... one by one... and they did a little fishing to remove stray shell fragments from the bowl. Faith mixed in the flour and buttermilk, while Philip greased the cake tin. Sal gave the mixture one final beat, smoothing out any lumps and they poured it into the pan; then slid it into the oven. While it was cooking, they had morning tea and cleaned up for the next part of the ritual. When the cake was brought out of the oven, they prepared the lemon sauce, by heating it gently over a low heat.

"I want to poke! I want to poke," shouted Philip enthusiastically.

"You did it last time. It's my turn," insisted Faith. "You will just make a mess. This is a special cake."

"Or perhaps the birthday girl can do it," offered Salome.

"This is a great honour that I accept," said Irene. "Since I have absolutely no idea what I'm doing, I think Faith should guide me as it is her turn." Faith beamed and very seriously, showed Irene how to hold the wooden spoon upside down, as Irene asked for a lot of reassurance from Philip, the other expert cake poker in attendance. Faith placed her hand over Irene's, and together they poked holes with the spoon handle into the cake, very carefully, in spaced lines. The ceremony and privilege of the occasion was not lost on Irene, and she 'ooed' and 'ahhed' through the ritual. Then the final act of culinary perfection was to pour the lemon sauce all over the cake and watched it seep into those deliciously poked holes. Philip was given the bowl and the spoon to lick. And Irene and Faith, started to plan how they would arrange the table for her birthday lunch.

* * *

When Flynn came in from the paddock, Simon was sitting with Irene on the verandah who was bouncing Daisy on her knee, both deep in conversation. Salome was inside fixing the salads and slicing the corned meat. She heard Flynn slap Simon on the shoulder as he went past. "I hope you are being respectful there, Mate, or a demotion is seriously on the cards."

"Always, Boss. Always," he said with a laugh.

Sal frowned. How could he joke about such a thing, when it was so obvious, what was happening? Was he blind? She was torn between her loyalty to Flynn, and her desire to continue to sabotage this event. But again, she turned away, gathered her wits, prepared a smile, and after Flynn had washed up and changed his shirt, she called everyone in for lunch.

Lunch was wonderful. They cut ragged slices of bread and sang happy birthday off-key. Faith ceremoniously presented the cake, and Irene cut it with a flourish. Irene announced it was the best birthday cake she had ever tasted.

After the table was cleared and the flowers Simon had brought for the birthday girl were placed back in the centre of the table, Philip started the parade of birthday gifts by presenting his wrapped present. Irene smiled, and shook it, and unwrapped... a rock. It was a special petrified-wood rock, one of Philip's greatest treasures. She assured him it would take pride of place on her teacher's desk as a paper weight. Faith presented a bookmark made from spare ribbon that came with her new dress, which went straight into the book Irene was reading. Flynn offered his gift of the elegant pen. So appropriate for a teacher. And Irene smiled and thanked him with an affectionate hug and a kiss on the cheek. Then Simon James presented his gift box... a beautiful bracelet, studded with amber topaz. Simon smiled and clasped it on her wrist and quietly disclosed this had been his mother's, given to her by his father when they were dating. The gasps of appreciation from the blushing Irene were matched only by the gasps of scandal from Salome. Would he dare to be more familiar with Mr Galloway's lady interest than Flynn himself? It seemed too shocking. Sal swallowed her embarrassment and went and made some tea.

She said little, washing dishes and clearing up while Irene went to pack her bags. It was agreed that Mr James would escort Irene back to town in the buggy, in order to catch the train, and Flynn would ride the saddle horse into Lenwick later in the evening, so Simon could leave for work first thing in the morning. Flynn had a few more jobs to do at home over the next a couple of days, and he gave Simon some other instructions before they left.

They all waved goodbye from the verandah. The children were irritable from their late night and big lunch, so Salome sent them both to bed with a book for an afternoon rest. They were soon asleep. She sat down in the lounge to feed Daisy. She was tired and wanted so much to sit back into her place of calm. But this time peace evaded her. She closed her eyes and tried not to cry.

* * *

18.

Flynn came and sat opposite her, stretching out on his chair, relaxed. "That seemed to go well. You know, I've had a wonderful couple of days."

Sal opened her eyes and looked at him sitting there, cool and naive. She frowned and wondered if she should burst his bubble. "Are you sure?"

"What do you mean? It was great. It seemed like the kids were having a great time too."

"But Simon James seems to be completely taken with Irene. Are you not disturbed by that?"

He grinned and shrugged. "I did say he was amiable, hardworking, and good looking. You have to agree... I was not wrong."

"But Flynn! Amber topaz is a symbol of deep love and affection. He gave her a bracelet full of it! One that had belonged to his mother! Surely you could not miss that?"

"I did not miss it. And if he had done less, I would have been talking to him. I vetted his interest right from the start. Irene could do much worse. No, I am content that they will make a fine couple, and my cousin will be happy."

Her eyes bugged out. "Your cousin?" she gasped.

"Yes, Irene is my cousin. Oh... You thought..." he said with a laugh. He seemed very amused.

"I only thought that because you wanted me to think that! Why wouldn't you tell me?"

He looked at her quietly for a moment. Then he looked down and traced the rough edges of the callouses across his palms. "I confess that I wanted to see if you might be a little protective of what we have here. But I have watched you carefully. Salome, the whole time Irene was here you have not faulted. You've been the most gracious and elegant hostess. There was not a flicker of distress. And I must say I feel slightly disappointed. I was hoping..."

When he looked up from studying his hands, he saw her face awash with hurt, tears on her lashes. Daisy was dosing off as she drank, and Sal was restrained by her presence to hold herself still. He looked at her, confused. "Salome? What is it?"

Her voice cracked. "I was so prepared to hate her. I wanted so much to scratch out her eyes in a green-eyed rage of spite; or sabotage her lovely nature to make her look poorly. I even manipulated seating arrangements and tried to distract you from disturbing Mr James from paying attention to her. I have fought and battled and reconciled myself to the disappointment that you have every right to love someone so charming. You deserve that. And yet... and yet... now you tell me she is your cousin! You brought her here to aggravate *me*? Well, your mission was accomplished Mr Galloway. It truly was! The entire time she was here, it was a visit of torment for me."

He was on the floor in front of her in a moment. "Oh Sal, forgive me! My comfort was that the kids were at least enjoying themselves. I had no idea! It seemed that you were indifferent to me."

"I have tried. Oh, I have tried. But Flynn, you are a not person for which indifferent will work. I thought... I have..." She took a shuddering breath in. "She is your cousin!"

"Yes, and I do love my cousin. Irene and I have been childhood friends, but she has had a series of unfortunate suitors, and she had all but given up. I told her she needed to choose more wisely... a quality person... someone like Simon James. I convinced Simon that they should write, and if he felt he wanted to meet after a period of correspondence then I would support them to do that. Sal, this weekend was primarily about them meeting up in person."

"So, this was all an act? But you have been completely irrational lately! I could have sworn you were in love!"

"Oh..." He swallowed hard, his Adam's apple bouncing in his throat. "Perhaps... but not with Irene. I had the idea that her being here would help me gauge if you might be open to considering... open to thinking of us, in a way that is more than our usual indifferent manner. Our lives are always wrapped up in practical matters and sorting through the busyness of life."

"Why not talk to me? Are we not good friends first?"

"I had planned so carefully how to tell you that my intentions were not about Irene. I had asked her to arrange it so that we could have a quiet dinner together. I wondered what it would be like to take you dancing – just the two of us; or talk by a campfire; or browse in a jewellery shop. I even brought you flowers. I wanted to experience these things... even if you were not in the mind to. The night she arrived... while you were serving dinner, I thought you were disturbed by her being here, but then you seemed so recovered I figured I misjudged it, so I left it alone. I was even hoping Irene might mistakenly expose my plan."

"Oh Flynn. What are you saying? I was your plan? For how long?"

"A while. I fell in love once... but this is different. This time it feels like I have 'walked into' love. My heart almost stops when I think about coming home and you not being here. And I know... I know you talk about your own home and your own independence, but as the time comes closer to Daisy's birthday, I am more and more agitated by the thought that you are going away... and you are taking Faith and Philip with you, and Daisy will lose her mother... again. Please Salome, please stay. Stay with me..."

"Stay? As your daughter's nanny... the caretaker of your animals... your housekeeper?"

"No! No! Don't you see? You are family. My family. You are. Stay Salome. Please. Marry me." His eyes searched her face.

"Oh Flynn..." She felt his breath as he leaned forward, drawing her in, and she kissed him. And he responded like on the dance floor. The moment twirled faster in time with their heartbeat, synchronised.

They felt Daisy squirm between them, and they released, staring at each other. "Thank you," he said. "Oh, thank you! It is good to know that Daisy will have you as her mother... forever. I have you forever."

She smiled bashfully and looked down at the baby between them. "But I didn't say yes."

"My heart knows a 'yes' when it hears it. You could not have yelled 'yes' any louder." And he kissed her again. "Oh, you were right Salome Frazer... we make so much sense."

* * *

They were still sitting together when the children woke up. Flynn called them over. "Hey Faith, Philip... come here for a tick, we want to tell you something."

The children sat seriously on the wooden chest that functioned as an occasional table in the room. Philip was pounding his legs against the sides of the box. Flynn suddenly found himself tongue-tied. Sal quickly spoke up.

"Do you remember how I have said that at the end of a year we would go back to our old house?" Philip objected... and Faith started to cry. "No, no... we want to tell you that has changed now. Flynn has asked us to stay. We are going to get married so this can be our home, and we get to keep each other." Philip was silenced and still. Faith's eyes miraculously dried. "We are going to stay here as a family," repeated Salome. "What do you think about that?"

Faith stared at them. "Weren't we family before? It felt like we were."

Philip stared at Daisy. "We don't have to give her back? That's better."

Faith's eyes didn't move. "When are you going to do that? Get married?"

Flynn returned her gaze and found his voice. "On Daisy's birthday. Yes, we will be married on Daisy's birthday," he said again as if confirming it to himself.

"Daisy's birthday?" repeated Salome. "That is just a month away."

"Why didn't you tell us this before now?" asked Faith.

"Because we weren't really sure until today," said Flynn with a reassuring smile.

Faith shook her head bewildered, rolled her eyes and stood up. "Adults. They never remember the important stuff. Can I go? I need to get my dress and shoes out. I have never been to a wedding before, and I have a lot to get ready." She stopped at the door and turned around. "Is this why we all got new outfits... for the wedding?"

Flynn shook his head. "No, I explained that. They were birthday presents, since you were sick when your birthdays came around. But I like the idea that we wear them for Daisy's birthday. That is a good idea. Except your mother... she gets to wear a special wedding dress."

"I do?"

Flynn grinned. "Maybe even one with a fashionable pleat?"

Faith shrugged her shoulders and left. Philip found his voice again. "Can I go and play now?" If this was sorted, then it didn't seem necessary that any of his plans should be interrupted.

"Sure. There are oatmeal biscuits on the table for afternoon tea." And they heard him explaining to Rusty on the verandah that he didn't need to be sad anymore, because he was going to stay here forever now. But Philip, of course, already knew that.

* * *

Salome took a deep breath and pushed her cup aside. "Daisy's birthday? Faith makes a good point. This is a very short engagement."

Flynn shrugged. "In a manner a speaking, the date was set a long time ago. You said that by Daisy's birthday I would either have a wife, or you would leave. I want to go with the wife option."

"But it is so soon, and you are going back to work, and there is... well... a lot to think about. Reverend Mason will want to talk to us both, given his concerns."

"I'll speak with Simon when I take his horse into town. He will look after things. We will just do what we do all the time: make a list and work through it together."

Sal nibbled on an oatmeal biscuit and brushed the crumbs aside, as she looked at the list of things Flynn was writing down. Flynn put down the pen and leant back. "I don't think you realise how much you have changed what it means being here," he said. "I wondered if I could even stay... after... you know, Joy... going. And if it wasn't for Daisy, I probably would not have stayed. It gave me a centre-point... being able to come back here... so I could see the kids, mess around with my animals, and just do normal stuff. Even this table. I never thought I would be sitting here planning our wedding."

"Well, I've always thought that a kitchen table is the hub of a home, like you said... the centre-point of where life happens."

Flynn went still and closed his eyes as a strange intense look crossed his face. "Or death..." he rasped quietly in a hoarse whisper.

"Flynn, what do you mean? Death...?" He pushed himself back from the table as he could no longer sit there. He paced around the room, disorientated for a moment. He quickly went out the door; it rattled hard against the doorjamb, closing sharply. She watched him stride over to the shed. "Faith? Keep an eye on Daisy. I'm going over to the shed."

"Yes Ma'ma."

Salome gently opened the shed door, and found Flynn grooming his horse, feverishly using a currycomb over his coat. "Flynn, are you okay?'"

"I will be..."

"What happened?"

He put down the currycomb as she touched his shoulder. He turned around and kissed her hard. Desperately. "Oh God... what if something happened to you? What if being married to me... meant..."

"You mean if I got pregnant?"

"I am not sure I can risk that. Before... it never occurred to me that being married was not forever. I never..."

"Flynn, you are right. We cannot know what the future holds." She reached out and touched his shirt, her fingers moving gently against his chest. "But I know one thing. I have no intention of living a celibate life when we marry. I've already had two children. It lowers the risk some. It will be fine."

"When you were talking about the kitchen table... it was like I was back there... the night Joy died. But it wasn't her on the table... it was you." He swallowed hard, and his face had turned ashen again.

Sal had only seen Flynn like that once before... the night Dr Mortimer had asked him to bring her to the infirmary so she could nurse Daisy. "Flynn... did Doc Mortimer lay Joy out on your kitchen table?"

A sob caught in his throat, and he nodded. "I planned to be back before she was due. But when I got home, she had already been labouring a long time. I fetched the Doc, but things just kept going wrong. They couldn't move her, and then they had to do a caesarean, post-mortem... to save Daisy's life. Sister Blaine said Daisy very nearly didn't make it..." His voice cracked into a sob.

"On the table? Your dining table? Oh God!" Sal swallowed and felt the shed spin sharply. She leant over, was sick, and passed out.

"Sal!" She heard someone calling to her from down a tunnel "Salome! Salome!" She stirred. She opened her eyes and looked into the terrified face of Flynn. He held her in his arms, where he sat on the floor of the shed. "Oh, thank goodness. You just went out."

She sat up. He pulled a tin cup down from a hook and dipped some water out of a bucket and handed it to her. Sal drank it slowly and said nothing for a long while. "I'm okay... I think."

He looked at her. "Are you sure? Does this change anything?"

She nodded and rubbed her forehead as she shifted her weight. "It changes a lot."

"Oh." He swallowed and felt his world tip.

"You know how I talk about the ragged edges of life? Well, this doesn't feel like that... this feels mutilated or damaged or irretrievable. Oh

Flynn... how did you do that? How did you let us sit at that table and watch us spread breakfast egg and toast crumbs, and finger-paints, and mashed veges, all over it?"

"I guess I was trying to forget. I didn't know how to say it. I'm sorry... I should have told you."

"Sorry? No! That's not what I meant. It must have been terrible for you! Your wife died there. You must have thought us so insolent... so disrespectful... so..." She shook her head as words failed her. "We just carried on as if everything was normal. It's disgraceful. Oh, I am so sorry! So sorry!"

"But you didn't know. How could you know? It was a comfort for it to be normal. It was. Salome... you and your family have brought peace back into my home."

She smiled gently and kissed him. "Now I know you are insane. Anyone who thinks Philip is peaceful is in denial."

"Oh Salome, I really love you. But I don't want to jeopardise you. I won't. Not this time. I'm supposed to protect you. I was supposed to protect Joy... and I didn't. If that means..." His eyes held fear again.

"It means I love you. That hasn't changed."

"But you said this does change things. Sal, will you still marry me? Even knowing this?"

She looked at him retreating, and she reached out and pulled him in, as if in some way he was teetering over a precipice, and she needed to hold him close to her. "There is no way that I am going to let Daisy have her birthday, without being your wife. You are a good man Flynn Galloway. We can do this..."

He held her close. "Thank God... it started to feel like death again."

"But..."

He studied her face, his brow furrowed. "But?"

"But... it's the table. I can't pretend I don't know that now. I cannot go in there and just allow the kids to smear gravy all over it, and spill their drinks, and squash their peas... and carry on. It feels so disrespectful. It should be a sacred space. It was where she died. It was where Daisy's life was saved."

"What do you want me to do? I won't be able to sell it. And it's too big to just push to the side."

"I don't know... but I *do* know I can't use it. Not now. I won't."

He sat for a while and then stood up resolutely and pulled his axe down from the rack on the wall. Salome followed him and put her hand on his forearm. She felt his muscles flex, tense with the resolution of action. "What if... what if we save the timber from the table. The cedar is so beautiful, so what if we make something... like a box? Maybe we could put Joy's jewellery in it... for Daisy when she turns twenty-one. We don't have to tell her what the box means... but it might be a way to honour what happened."

Flynn nodded.

Sal swallowed. "And I wondered... did Joy have a favourite tree? We could plant a tree in the back yard... for shade."

"You are thinking of a climbing tree for the kids, aren't you?"

"I am."

"Well, she was rather partial to Mrs Trimboli's mulberry pie..."

"A mulberry tree is perfect."

* * *

19.

Reverend Mason took a moment before he ushered them into the vestry. "I trust you realise that this does nothing to assuage the sins of the past year."

Salome held Flynn's hand firmly as she felt it flex. "Reverend. We want to be married, regardless of what the last year has looked like. We cannot fix the past but are looking towards the future."

He paused, and then he could contain himself no longer. He burst into a tirade of their responsibility to be a good example to their children, and their children's children, and that life needed to be taken seriously. Reverend Mason preached fire and brimstone as if to a congregation of a hundred, and the noise became like crickets and cicadas humming at dusk in their ears.

"Mr Galloway? Mr Galloway, do you understand what I have said?"

"Oh. Well, I think I have got the gist of it, yes."

"And Mrs Frazer? Do you also understand?"

Salome nodded and tried not to think that she might not be telling the whole truth in the house of God.

"I will need to meet with you again before the wedding."

"Really? What for?"

"This is so you understand the sacrament of marriage. It is what I do for all my parishioners before their nuptials."

"But we both have been married before."

"Obviously it has not held you in good stead... if you are back here. Marriage is meant...."

"Surely you don't blame us for our spouses dying Reverend. We are not responsible for their untimely deaths."

"Well, only God can judge. I can book the church on the day you request. But not until late afternoon. That's all I can offer. And..."

"Yes. Thank you, Reverend, for your time," said Salome quickly. "An afternoon wedding is fine. Unfortunately, I have another appointment now, so we must be going."

They walked out, and Flynn helped Sal climb into the cart. He sat there loosely holding the reins and ran his hand through his hair. "The man is a pompous fool. I hardly think it is possible that God has got his hand on this."

"Remember the ragged edges? Those are the times when God has helped me. I prayed that my house would be saved... so that my children would have a home... and you agreed to our arrangement, even when it went against everything you wanted. That felt like the hand of God."

"Huh. Well, okay. I prayed Daisy would be safe despite my stubborn disregard of your advice, and that you would help her, even when I had seriously blown any chance of you being willing to do so... and yet you did. Without hesitation."

Salome nodded and smiled. "I prayed that Irene would fall off a cliff and drown in the ocean... which she didn't... and that might be because we live a long way from the sea. I even prayed you were not really in love, but I find out you were. And even though my prayer was not answered... it was, because you love me. I find it hard to say even now: you love me. That is the miracle. The God who answers our prayers, even when we pray in awkward and uninformed ways... his hand is with us."

"Huh. Remind me not to get on the wrong side of your praying knees."

"Mason thinks he is helping God... but one man, with his own ideas about God, doesn't make them true. God will help us to be gracious and kind in the ragged edges of life, even if Reverend Mason doesn't have a mind to. So, we will sit through his awful presentations... and then we will be married. Right now, I am due to have a fitting for a wedding dress, an activity which tradition dictates you cannot participate in."

"Well, I'll drop the table off at Henrik's Workshop and meet you here in an hour. If anyone can make a beautiful jewellery box out of tragedy, I think Henrik will be the one."

"That sounds like the hand of God too."

Finally, they sat down with coffee cups at Mrs Trimboli's place and Sal kicked off her shoes. Mrs Trimboli clucked and fussed and then burst into tears. "Oh, my darlings!" she gushed when they shared their news and asked if she would help. "How I have hoped and prayed you both would see what was before you. Oh... it is my pleasure!" Mrs Trimboli quickly activated her family to host the birthday-wedding breakfast... in the late afternoon. Flynn's reassurances that they only needed simple refreshments and a birthday cake for Daisy, fell on deaf ears.

* * *

The day arrived so quickly. To satisfy Reverend Mason, when Flynn came back from work, he took up residence in Mrs Trimboli's spare room until the wedding. That was easier than packing up three children. He rode out to the farm each morning and they continued to work through their preparations. He arrived earlier on the wedding morning to welcome Daisy to her first birthday with a special breakfast. They watched her unwrap

143

presents and then they all went through the bath like cattle plunging through a river crossing. Then they piled into the buggy to change into their wedding clothes at Mrs Trimboli's house. Irene had arrived to be Salome's attendant, and Simon was to stand with Flynn as a witness.

Faith and Irene held a bouquet of poppies and ivy from their own garden as they walked down the aisle of the church; Philip carried the rings tied securely on a cushion borrowed from Mrs Trimboli's daughter-in-law; Daisy stayed with Flynn at the altar and charmed everyone with her one-year-old song. He handed Daisy over to Irene, and then turned to see Salome enter. Her dress was an elegant blue, even with a couple of flattering pin tucks across the bodice, her arms filled with poppies and ivy... the blooming of peace. Reverend Mason said his piece; and the couple said their vows. Most of the guests present were Mrs Trimboli's family and they sighed in appreciation. There were those who refused to attend who tut-tutted as they looked at their mantle-clocks and muttered that it was about time that they "did the right thing".

When they arrived at Mrs Trimboli's house just on dusk, a series of long trestle-tables ran across the yard. There were candles in jars along the centre of the table, and all around the edge of her vegetable patch, and hanging off the fences on wire hooks.

"Oh," cried Faith. "It is so pretty. They look just like fireflies!"

They feasted on Italian pastas and risottos. Irene had brought her violin to play a waltz for the bride and groom. As they danced, Flynn quietly asked with a smile, "Will I escape being trampled this evening by my dance partner?"

"Depends on whether you are going to spend your time talking about your cousin," responded Salome with a smile.

"Well... my bride has all my attention tonight." They danced without any missteps, with a lot of smiles, and a breathless kiss at the end.

Someone came forward to give Irene a break at playing, and Simon quickly held out his hand to capture her for the next dance, or three. Faith danced with Flynn and then one of the Trimboli cousins stepped in to dance with Faith. Philip went missing, which activated a frantic search. He was found sitting in the henhouse, in his good clothes, talking to the chooks who had already settled into roost. He was explaining to them about their permanent adoption into the Trimboli family, because they were staying at the farm. Then it was time for Daisy's birthday cake. She sat in her highchair and proceeded to smear cake all over herself and anyone who challenged her ability to demolish this wonderfully delicious dessert.

* * *

20.

So, the day drew to a close, like a gentle curtain falling. Flynn's buggy was adorned with tin cans filled with stones and rag streamers. They drove out of town in a flurry of well wishes. As they pulled up outside the front of the house, Flynn drew his wife in for a kiss. "Welcome home Mrs Galloway."

"Flynn, I don't even know how this happened. Didn't you say that you and me... we were never going to happen?"

"Hmm, I think I might have said that. I'm grateful I was mistaken."

"You said I was never in the running..."

"Yesss... much like you said that you didn't want a husband, and you would never expose your children to my rudeness."

Salome shook her head amazed. "I didn't understand then how much your grief was talking. So many things have changed, and I hardly know when it was different. When did it change?"

"Slowly. Months of life. Months and months of the ragged edges of life. You have shown me Salome, that so much of life is offered in the ragged edges... the rough, uneven, uncomfortable... sad times. Whenever I found the house looking like it had been hit by an earthquake, I was frustrated and angry. Then one day I came home and found the house in absolute chaos, worse than I had ever seen it. You were slumped on the lounge, completely exhausted, sick as a dog, nursing Daisy, both of you covered in spots. You were fighting for her so hard that you didn't even realise you were sick yourself. You did that, even though you knew you would walk away at the end of the year." He reached out and caressed a chickenpox scar on her temple. "That moment punched some sense in to me. It winded me completely. That was when I determined that you shouldn't fight for my family alone. I needed to step up. I didn't want you to do it alone, and I didn't want to do it without you."

She chuckled. "And here I was assuming it was my animal husbandry skills, or my excellent cooking."

"Ahh... the way you look tonight, Mrs Galloway, that alone would get you over the line. You are so beautiful. I am astounded that I never saw you to start with."

"I am flattered Flynn Galloway... and a little amazed myself that I didn't see you either. I'm glad both our eyes have been opened."

"Sal, which ragged edge moment changed your dogged determination not to like me? Come, one confession deserves another."

"I think it began early on... when I didn't even realise. You gave your word, and even though you really didn't see any value in it, you worked hard on my house. On your days home, you crawled around under my house, covered in dust and cobwebs. Every time you bumped your head and cursed, I expected you to bail, and yet you kept leveling that house so that my family... a family you didn't even know, could live there more comfortably. You did that, even when everyone around was judging you for making choices that were not even true. You transformed my inadequate, unattractive dump of a house into the beautiful little cottage that it is now, and that started to transform what I saw in you. I confess, part of me is disappointed that I won't get to live there now."

"We could move there if you prefer," he said with a grin.

"Nah... we will manage with living here at Bottlebrush Grove."

"Salome, I once promised I would not gamble with your family home. I meant that. Just because we are married, that little house is still yours, and the income it brings, is yours as well."

She chuckled. "Well, I'm sure that will confuse Mr Symanski a great deal, since we now have a marriage certificate."

He lifted his bride down and carried her up the stairs, across the verandah, and over the threshold into their home as husband and wife. He stopped at the table and lit the lamp. There was a new table, an oval table, the golden grain of silky oak shimmering in the lamplight. It stood there, inviting them to create a new centre-point, a new hub for their marriage and family. Salome smiled as she followed the polished grain of the wood with her hand. This table was the perfect centre to revolve around their family life ... a place where love and laughter and tears would be felt as the ragged edges of life would come.

"Welcome home Mrs Salome Ivy Galloway," he whispered.

On the table was a gift, wrapped simply in white paper with blue ribbon... the colours of peace. She unwrapped it carefully. It was a cedarwood jewellery box, the lid beautifully carved with poppies and ivy leaves. Sal traced the engraving with her fingers. "Oh, this is beautiful! So beautiful."

"When you told me your bouquet would be poppies and ivy, the flowers of peace, I couldn't resist. Henrick worked hard on it to have it ready." She reached up and removed her single string of pearls, simple and elegant, which had belonged to Joy and were her wedding gift from Flynn. She circled them around, inside the lined box, and enveloped Flynn in an embrace.

He held her in his arms. "So apparently ivy is a hardy plant that not only represents peace but strong, enduring love... a beautiful complement to the fragile petals of poppies," he said. "I hope Bottlebrush Grove will always feel like home for you. This was a place of Joy for me once... and I know now that regardless of the challenges we might face as a family, there is also a peace that is resilient and hardy."

Sal sighed. Flynn was right... their life at Bottlebrush Grove, would be marked by gathering around this table together; to remind each other the ragged edges are covered with God's overarching love and peace.

***

The end

Other books by this author

Matt's Boys of Wattle Creek
Maggie & Minotaur
Rose's Diary

Gems of Australia Series:
Sapphires of Hope
Rubies of Ambition
Emerald Dreams

Homes of Healing Series:
The Beachside Cottage
Petra Downs
The Writer's Retreat

Guthrie's Lot Series:
A Spacious Place
A Level Path
The Crying Tree

Pioneers of Grace Series:
Time of Grace
Circle of Grace
Journey of Grace
Mask of Grace
Crucible of Grace

Sculpture of Grace

The Bottlebrush Grove Series
Shadows in the Corners
The Ragged Edges
Scratches across the Surface
Cracks through the Core

Children's Book
The Bush Olympics.

www.ingramcontent.com/pod-product-compliance
Lightning Source LLC
Chambersburg PA
CBHW051705180726
48283CB00004B/1221